Saturday Night
at SARAH JOY'S

wash

cut

drink

eat

talk

lather

reload

repeat

Saturday Night
at Sarah Joy's

by John Allison

INFINITY
PUBLISHING

Copyright © 2012 by John Allison
Cover image credit: Wallenrock/Shutterstock.com

ISBN 978-0-7414-8014-9 Paperback
ISBN 978-0-7414-8015-6 eBook
Library of Congress Control Number: 2012917311

Printed in the United States of America

Published January 2013

INFINITY PUBLISHING
1094 New DeHaven Street, Suite 100
West Conshohocken, PA 19428-2713
Toll-free (877) BUY BOOK
Local Phone (610) 941-9999
Fax (610) 941-9959
Info@buybooksontheweb.com
www.buybooksontheweb.com

A Personal Letter from the Author to You

You should be asking yourself some questions about this book—questions such as "Why should I read this book?" "What is this book about?" and "Why would someone write this book?" If those are the questions that *you* came up with as well (on your own, not copying from anyone), good job! We're going to get along well. Let me comment here, possibly addressing these questions.

A good place to begin is the title. The story takes place, for the most part, in a salon called The Conscilience, owned and operated by a woman named Sarah Joy. Like most normal people you run into with your cart at the Food King, she's an interesting person, one worth getting to know. She has this in common with most of the other characters you will meet.

Since this letter is an unlikely place to introduce her to you, I will. Characters in stories usually don't come alive to the reader until the storyteller provides a description. Since this is a work of fiction, perhaps you can take a moment to picture your own Sarah Joy. When you leave her salon, you're looking forward to the next time you see her. What would that person look like to you? Who could give you the hint of a head and neck massage before your haircut begins, and make you feel special and appreciated? Who would you feel completely comfortable talking to? Perhaps you just need to picture a face—one that you can look in the eye. Perhaps you just need to picture a smile. Can you imagine a laugh so infectious that, if you heard it, you could find its owner in a crowded room? Can you feel the touch of two hands on your shoulders that makes you instantly relax and look forward to an hour of pampering and good conversation? This should be all the description you need to get started.

Since we're discussing a beauty salon, realize that, by the time you finish this book, you will think differently about them. You will have a template for operating a successful business. If you are a salon owner, you'll come up with many new ideas for your own place. If you're someone who has hair and gets it cut, you'll be pissed that so little is done where you go, so you'll be pointing out their shortfalls from now on. Keep thinking about what more can be done where you get your hair cut, to get them closer to the ultimate (Sarah Joy's). There is a sea of ideas to sail in here for you.

In further dissecting the title, the phrase "Saturday Night" appears. On some Saturday nights, when Townsend's Florists is closed, when Sheffield's Drugs and Sundries is snoring, and when Just Lamps is dark for the day, The Conscilience is open for business by appointment only. Regulars are scheduled in, frequently as couples. Friends work to secure the four or more time slots; then they all show up at 5 PM with wine and cheese, and settle in for a special evening. Not many people, I would guess, develop social situations around getting one's hair done as extensively as do some of the Saturday night groupies at Sarah Joy's. It's a night for talking and imbibing. Sarah Joy knows how to be the catalyst to make everyone talk a little too much. Usually that makes the night even more fun, or so I'm told.

I heard some male eyes roll when I told you that the story takes place in a salon, possibly suggesting that this book is written primarily for female readers. This is, honestly, BS. If you've ever gotten your hair cut, this book is for you. I know a woman (unidentified) who was reading the book and enjoying it—until she made the mistake of sharing a few paragraphs with her husband. *She's* now waiting to finish the book because her husband stole it and *he's* reading it! I rest my case: this book is not written for "the ladies". This leads to my advice. For your personal sanity—*buy two copies* right from the start, and squelch the endless arguments that erupt when there's only one copy in the bedroom. While the book has not even been printed at the time of this writing, there are rumors that some small Caribbean countries are actually requiring that the book be sold in pairs! I should also point out that it is the perfect book to be read anywhere—whether you're cuddled up by the fire, on break at work, "working" at work, or by the pool! No, I don't have a pool either, but with your help ...

As the new owner of two copies of this book, with no questions asked concerning how you got them, you have a few assignments. Your first task, realizing that this is pure fiction (wink), is to determine where the salon and Sarah Joy are. You probably know someone who knows someone who goes there. There are certainly enough hints. The second assignment, for you to ponder while you're getting your money's worth in terms of meeting characters, is to think about who may be "the bad guy" in the last chapters. While this is largely a "slice of life" kind of story, with no particular beginning or ending, it also may be more. The end of the story contains the following lines (at least they were in a rough draft, I believe):

> No one heard the door open. Sarah Joy was the first to notice the business end of a shotgun coming into her styling room from the main entrance. She raised her hand to silence the group, and they all froze. That shotgun was attached to a very unhappy-looking ...

I feel obligated to warn you that this is a bit of a whodunit: not a typical whodunit, but there *is* a moment when you know there's a gun but you don't know who's holding it—a moment of suspense, confusion, or personal satisfaction if you are anticipating whose finger is on the trigger. I just hate it when writers spring stuff like this on you late in the book and you feel like you need to read it over again, so I'm telling you now. Also, I promise it probably won't be the guy who is introduced on page 901, who stopped by asking for directions, one page before he returns with an attitude. Keep this in mind as you get to know some of the characters. I'd recommend that you just be suspicious of everyone you encounter—in this book as well.

Thank you for spending some time with all of us whom you are about to meet. We're glad you're here. Did you bring any wine? Great!

But seriously ...

Textbooks instruct writers on the importance of creating strong protagonists and antagonists when writing fiction. The story *must* have a pivotal character who wants something more than anything else, and a strong opponent who becomes a dangerous foe. Certainly much exciting and dramatic fiction follows such writing rules. I prefer to live a slice of *life* with the characters who appear when I write. *Life*—where you get to know the good from the bad by how they act and how they live. *Life*—where, if you participate, you'll find that ordinary people can do amazing and surprising things. It's easy to develop the story of a hero, different to appreciate that average people in life can rise to become a hero at any moment—or an antihero. For every hero who makes the news, there are thousands who quietly do what needs to be done, usually surprising even themselves.

I hope you will enjoy getting to know the special, average people in this book—except, perhaps, for one or two.

Contents

* Bonus tracks; not available on the album.

- 0 -

JUST SOME PAPERWORK

MEMORANDUM
from the desk of Jeanne Burton, A.R.

To: Eric Ruggles, Co-Owner
        American Realty Company
From: Jeanne Burton
        Assistant Realtor
RE: 8114 Spruce Lane Property

Of course, Eric, I am pleased to tackle any and all opportunities to sell real estate in this area, and the above-mentioned property is certainly real. Let me remind you of the situation there. It was at one time a lovely house with unique, probably stunning, classic lines, but when the Anderson family inherited both it and the house next door, the shit quite literally hit the fan. I don't know if the husband or wife worked, but they quickly got into trouble for unpaid taxes, unpaid utility bills, cancelled credit cards, etc. The police responded to numerous calls from concerned neighbors when the Anderson children would play in, and lie on, the street at all hours. I don't know if their dogs were hunting dogs or something "special," but the decision to use the second property—the one that I am now supposed to sell—as a doghouse is inconceivable to me. The dogs "did their business" on the once-beautiful wood floors, which surely contributed to the bugs and rats that live inside the walls. One of the brighter Andersons apparently kicked out a few windows so the dogs could get in and out. Even this they could not do well. All of the broken windows had glass shards remaining in them. The dogs and whatever other visitors who came to party must have been frequently cut by the sharp glass either in the window frames or outside on the ground, because there is a substantial blood pattern on the floor, from the windows to every corner of the house. Too bad no one ever went inside to notice.

We have paid to have piles of dog feces removed and some other unsavory items attended to, but I don't see this property moving until someone, probably us, gets it back into some minimally decent shape. We should at least put windows back into the first floor and have the floors redone. Dried blood has historically not been an attractive feature for a house on the market.

I have had one person call and ask to see the property. She saw it—actually walked inside. She spent time looking around. Obviously she could not imagine what had happened there. Before she left, she took a pad of post-it notes out of her purse, wrote a number on one, and handed it to me. I'm guessing it was a receipt for lunch at McDonald's, not an offer on the property. However, this is no ordinary property, so who knows. I was too embarrassed to ask what it was, since I was doing my best to try not to breathe and to brush bugs off both of us, so I hope she'll call me. I'm not holding my breath (ha ha).

I'm rambling, as you always say I do. I'll just restate my request that a budget be established for cleaning up the property, and I'll point out that whatever you decide, it's ridiculously too little, too late. If you know someone who can replace the windows, please let them know that there is probably a fox living in the basement, and I'm pretty sure he's pissed. He expected better accommodations.

- 1a -

INTRODUCTIONS

The Conscilience recently grew to a total permanent staff count of three, not including several others who work a day a week, or are on call for the holidays. Grace has been working as a stylist and front-desk manager of The Conscilience for two years, and some believe that one day Sarah Joy will turn the business over to her. A week ago William was hired to develop a massage offering and to do things that need to be done. (Sometimes you just need a man around the house.) William had been thrown into the fire—he hadn't even been given a tour of the salon and was already unloading a delivery truck! All part of the plan. Sarah Joy wanted William to get his own sense of the salon; then she wanted Grace and William to spend some time together—hopefully to bond, maybe even develop some plans and ideas of their own. Grace and William agreed to gather on this Sunday morning, meeting at 9:00 AM in the salon. Of course, Grace was there at 8:00 AM. Sarah Joy claimed that she needed to spend the morning shopping so "the kids" could speak freely without Big Sister listening in.

Grace has a serious hippy spirit and is refreshing to be around. With a wave, Sarah Joy walked out the front door. Grace didn't notice—she was in her own little world, enjoying the space of the big front room of the salon, listening to the music in her head, humming. With eyes closed, she Stevie Nicks-ed around the place in one of her signature long skirts. Sarah Joy looked at her through the window—another day, another hair color, another hairstyle. *Grace was such a find!* Sarah Joy smiled.

Grace heard William's car pull into the parking lot. She checked the clock. 8:45. She didn't need any more information. William was going to work out just fine. Any other indicator might not lead a person to the same conclusion. He just didn't look like a match for a beauty salon. He had come to the US from Cuba in his early teens with a family member. Pure Cuban stock, William is a little Mac Truck—short, muscular, and ready for anything. He was told that his job was to keep the place stocked and clean. He is also going to the University part-time, evenings, studying computer science. William will be doing chair massages, a new addition to the salon's offerings, although he had no customers in his first week.

William shyly stood at the front door, not knowing if he should knock, but when he saw Grace coming to meet him, he opened the door.

"Well, new boy," Grace teased him, "your first week is over. Guess it's about time you got the tour of this place!"

William smiled. "That would be wonderful. I had no idea what I was doing last week. I didn't know where anything was or where to put things."

"Don't worry, I'll take care of you." Grace patted him on the head. "We have a lot to do this morning. We should spend some time talking about how Sarah Joy works. You and I need a plan for how *we're* going to run this place, but first I'm just psyched to officially show you around!"

Grace twirled around, pointing to the room around them. "Physically, Sarah Joy designs around themes—themes on top of themes, themes embedded in themes. So you tell me. What do *you* see? What do *you* want to know about? You can start the tour, Master William!"

Why doesn't anyone just do anything simply here? William thought. *I'm the new guy so I'm going to start the tour? Women!* Still, he appreciated the challenge.

William picked up a hairbrush, surprising even himself as he spoke into it, attempting his very best Robin Leech.

"We're here today in the beautiful Conscilience Salon in sunny ..."

"No, no, no," Grace interrupted. "It's not the Conscilience Salon. It's The Conscilience. Period."

William started again. "We're here today in The Conscilience Period. Obviously at one time it was a large and beautiful home; the first floor is now a salon. The owner, Sarah, lives in understated elegance upstairs."

"Sarah Joy," Grace said. "Don't ask me why, but for some reason most people call her 'Sarah Joy.' Maybe it's because her last name sounds like a middle name—you know, like 'Billy Bob'? I can't explain it, but it's always safe to call her Sarah Joy."

Happy to be getting this level of detail, William continued to Leech. "One cannot help but notice the beauty of the great room that we stand in, which stretches across the front of the house. The wood trim and cabinetry, all painted a bright and fresh stark white, pop in the morning sun."

"But not the floors," Grace added.

"Yes, I can see the floors are not white, Grace," William acknowledged. "I'll try to be more exact for the listeners." He squinted at her, staring her down. Grace gasped, then picked up another brush and whacked him. William winced, but continued.

"The floors are a beautiful light wood, refinished to a high gloss—almost like one incredible mirror! Most of the outer walls on the first floor are windows—massive windows. They add to the special feel of the front room. Many features—I mean 'layers,' grab the attention of those who come in the front door. All of the walls are a deep purple. It works well. It makes the whole salon pop!" William said.

"What's the big deal with the purple? You don't think it could be white? A pastel? What's so special about purple?" Grace asked, pushing him.

William looked around, thinking about what the paint did to the room. "Well, to me it makes it different ... special. You wouldn't find a house painted like this. So while it is a house, you know you're somewhere else. In a business. Yeah, that's it!"

Grace smiled, very impressed. She even put her brush down, and waved at him to continue.

"The front room is impressive in size, yet sparsely decorated. We have the colorful checkout counter by the door. There is a Franklin stove that feeds into the fireplace at one end of the room between two large windows.

"Wait—does that stove get used in the winter?" he interrupted himself to ask her. "It's a very nice piece, but there's no wood or implements or anything around it."

"I've never seen it used," Grace told him, "but I love it too. Doesn't it just make you feel warm?"

William nodded, then continued his brush broadcast.

"One can't ignore almost a whole wall of glass shelves displaying Aveda products."

He turned to Grace, holding his hand over the brush so no one would hear. "Is this stuff for real? How many creams do you need for your face? I mean, 'ear lobe cream'! Really?"

"We don't have ear lobe cream!" Grace argued.

William pointed to the top shelf. Grace gasped. "Oh, 'evening ear lobe cream.' Well, of course. You have to be specific. Yes, we have lots of things for people to purchase. When your life is filled with Aveda products, you feel good. Sarah Joy makes a lot of money on this stuff, and on the jewelry and things that some local artists make and she stocks, so be careful not to criticize."

"Yes, dear," William said. He froze, not believing he'd called her "dear." It just popped out. He was being silly. Grace picked up her brush and whacked him again. Tension over.

"There are shelves close to the ceiling all the way around the room that hold her collection of old-lady hats," William continued.

"Hold it right there, buddy," Grace interrupted. "Two items: first, you haven't finished with the room furnishings, and second, we're gonna need to talk about your phrase, 'old-lady hats.'"

"Uh, OK," William said. He looked around. "Oh, there is a very sweet massage chair where your masseur, William, will be providing massages."

"I hope so," Grace said. "It would be a good extra income line for the salon."

"Oh, I'm going to take the job of developing regular clients very seriously," William assured her. "Probably I'll offer some free mini-chair massages to clients and see what comes of it. I want to put something on the website too."

"How does a computer science major become a masseur?" Grace asked.

"My first college major was sports nursing," William explained. "I learned everything I needed to know in my first two years. Can we get back to the old-lady hats now?"

Grace sighed. "I'm sure the old ladies will appreciate your description. I know it's what they are, but please realize that they're an important part of this place to Sarah Joy. She's been collecting them since she was young. Some of them are her aunt's hats. Each one comes with a name and a story, and she knows them all."

"Oh, yes, the stories. She tells them too!" William said. "I listened to her talk about one hat all day. Every time she had a new client, the story changed just a bit.

Grace smiled. "Must have been Hat Tuesday. Yes, sometimes they do seem to have a life of their own. Some of them are just beautiful, I think. Still, I want you to be careful. You can call them 'old *lady hats*,' but not '*old lady* hats,' OK?"

William was grateful that he lived in a place where italics were so easy to hear. He raised his brush microphone again and continued. "Across the back half of the house, we have two styling rooms, each accessible from the front room; and in the middle is a staircase that, uh, goes upstairs. Next to the staircase is a small hallway that leads to the back of the house, and also holds two doors:

one to the basement, and one to the bathroom. OK, Grace, what did I miss?"

"You're doing great, William," Grace said. "Sarah Joy's styling room is on one side—the side that gets the most sun—and my room is on the other side. It's nice that they are separated, so conversations stay local. And if we do happen to have a loud customer ... " Grace walked over to a blank section of wall and lightly touched it. A panel popped open. She reached inside, and suddenly background music began to play.

"Oh, that's sweet," William said.

"Yes, it is," Grace agreed, "but hands off. The decision on background music for privacy is Sarah Joy's choice alone. House rules. I think she likes to have control because the music she selects depends on which two customers are here."

William nodded.

"OK," Grace continued. "Go into each of the salons and tell me what you see. What's the same, what's different? This is your real test."

William walked through each one, commenting as he walked. "Purple and white again. Sparse again. Each room has a chair for washing hair, with a little washbowl behind it, and then there's a separate barber chair for cutting. Each room has a wall that is mostly a big mirror. More big windows. Bright, bright everywhere. Sparse. Two chairs and one little white bureau that holds clippers and combs, blow dryers, brushes.

"They're pretty much the same ... but not," he continued.

"What's different?" Grace pushed him.

"I don't know! It's really strange. They're mirror images but they're different." William spun and spun around, going back and forth between the two rooms. "I know something's different! Can you just tell me?"

William hadn't pointed out an important difference—that Sarah Joy's salon had a small hallway that led directly to the storage room, where he would often sit and eavesdrop.

Grace whacked him with her brush.

"What was that for?" William yelped.

"Not sure," Grace replied. "So you give? Look closely at the walls. Same purple, but Sarah Joy's are shinier—like a high gloss in her room, a semigloss in the rest of the salon. Interesting, don't you think? Her room is different."

"Funny," William mused. "You think she did that on purpose?"

"Everything here is done on purpose, William," Grace grinned. "We're doing good here. You know that in the back there's a storage room. I think they used to call it a 'mud room.' I'm sure you've put a lot of stock back there. Keep a list of what you have, or label the boxes or something. You'll be glad you did. There's also some chairs in there, and a portable hair dryer for perms and color jobs."

"Yes, I noticed. All old office chairs, on wheels," William said. "What's that about?"

"I'll get to them, don't worry," Grace assured him. "Anything else?"

"Well ... the basement! Geez. I spend a lot of time down there," William said.

"Seriously?" Grace asked him. "What do you do down there?"

"Try to keep busy," he replied. "There is a constant flow down to the basement of towels and those sheet things people wear ..."

"Smocks," Grace interrupted.

"Smocks, OK," William nodded. "So I've been washing, drying, and folding smocks every day. I make coffee all day, and try to keep the ice machine running and the fridge full of the soda pop that she stocks. I'm usually either there or in the storage room."

"Poor William; what a lonely life," Grace said, making a big frowny face.

"Not really. When I'm up here, I'm listening to Sarah Joy, and when I'm downstairs ... I have lots of company. You know, all those creepy Styrofoam heads with the old wigs on them? And more hats, of course. When I get bored, I make up names for the disembodied heads and talk to them."

William paused. "I probably shouldn't have told you that. Think I'm a weirdo?" he asked.

"Definitely," Grace was quick to respond. "That's why you're gonna work out so well here." She smiled. "Plus you used the word 'disembodied.' I like that! Good job on the tour. We have lots of things to talk about, but the other day I found something that might be worth reading. Sarah Joy keeps a little scrapbook for the salon. There's some interesting things in it—might be fun to look at. Want to see it?"

Grace sat in her styling room's barber chair with the book in her lap, and William rolled an office chair in from the back room to sit next to her and see what they could learn.

THE SCRAPBOOK

Grace and William sat down with Sarah Joy's scrapbook between them. Two items about the salon were of particular interest—both from the *City Magazine*, a publication that covers local topics and issues.

Taken from the *City Magazine*, "The Inside Word on the Area's Top Salons," April Issue.

Easily overlooked but not to be ignored in this town's hair styling offerings is the up-scale and visually beautiful Conscilience (8114 Spruce). Understated style accompanies hair, skin, and nail care that clients love. *You* know someone who goes there for everything from Aveda products to great cuts and new looks, and they're undoubtedly loyal. The owner lists education and consulting in her services. Accessible parking, friendly staff, and outstanding, consistent cuts, perms, and color make this salon a gem. Mon.–Sat. by appointment, (888) 555-9534.

The second item that they found interesting was also from the *City Magazine*. There is a regular section that appears on the last page or two of every issue called "Ten Questions," where a *City Mag* reporter interviews a local person of interest, often a new member of the business community. In this issue, "Ten Questions" was dedicated to Sarah Joy!

Ten Questions for Sarah Joy
New Salon Owner and Operator

C.M. We're pleased to be speaking with Sarah Joy, a recent addition to our area. She just opened a wonderful new salon on Spruce Street—The Conscilience. Welcome!

S.J. Thank you for highlighting my shop! I haven't been in the area very long, but I've found the *City Magazine* to be very informative. I always look forward to the next issue.

C.M. Great! As you know, this part of the magazine is called ten questions, so let's get started. *Q#1.* Can you tell us a little about the actual salon—The Conscilience?

S.J. The Conscilience used to be a beautiful residential property—the kind of house you'd see in the movies. The salon is painted with a bright white on all of the woodwork, and a bright purple on the walls. I think the colors really make it a fun, vibrant place to visit. We have two styling rooms and two stylists.

C.M. *Q#2.* How in the world did you settle on such an unusual name—the "Conscilience"? Is it a real word?

S.J. Yes, it is, almost! I spent a few weeks in our lovely city library considering everything from poem titles to Latin phrases to just making up an interesting-sounding word.

Purely by accident, I stumbled on a very old book, published in 1840. William Whewell discussed the problem of how academic areas of study rarely benefit from each other, but at some point, we need to find a way to bring disconnected areas together so that new knowledge and theories can be created. He called the process of bringing many ideas together into a single common groundwork "consilience." It was just the idea I was looking for, because I try to provide the best service to a wide variety of clients.

C.M. Wow! And some places go with names like "Just Cuts." (laughs) *Q#3.* What is the best thing about your salon?

S.J. When you come to us, professionals treat you with respect while you have your hair done, styled, cut, colored, or have something new created. We work to make The Conscilience a relaxing place that offers something for all kinds of clients. One way we do this is to not rush in our work. We schedule a full hour or more for each client, as needed. We work hard to provide substantial service, both to our customers and to the neighborhood as well.

C.M. *Q#4.* What is the worst thing about your salon?

S.J. Can't this just be called "Three Questions"? (laughs) Well, we ... I still have a few things to work out. Just today, one of my good clients asked me, for the tenth time, why I don't put a few nice sofas in the front room of the salon as a waiting room. I told him that I didn't want a waiting room because my goal is to never have anyone wait! Of course, my appointment before him had run a little over, and I found him in our massage chair! I certainly get his point, but I'm going to find a way to guarantee that clients never have to wait, so I'm holding off on the furniture.

C.M. *Q#5.* Like many salons, I assume you carry some product line. Can you tell us about that part of the business?

S.J. A good part of the front room, which runs the width of the entire house, is dedicated to Aveda products. We sell creams, shampoos, aromatherapy candles, hardware—such as brushes and hair dryers—and a rich selection of jewelry, scarves, and sundries from local artists.

C.M. We have some "personal" questions that we try to ask everyone who appears in "Ten Questions." So here we go. *Q#6.* Can you tell us something about Sarah Joy, the person?

S.J. These are tough! Well, I love what I do because I don't just cut hair—I take care of people. I tell stories; I listen to them. My clients are all very important to me, and I honestly do think of them as my family. If I hadn't learned to cut hair, I'd probably be working in a hospital or nursing home, doing the same thing—finding ways to take care of people. It's just what I do, and I think I do it well.

C.M. *Q#7.* All of the employees who work for *City Magazine* live in the city. The editors think this is important, and the staff agrees. Could you tell us where you live and why you chose it?

S.J. Well, I should get some points for this! I drive zero miles to work every morning. I live where I work. The house is a big one, so the salon is downstairs, and I live upstairs. There's actually no separation. There is an open staircase that leads from my main hallway to the center of the salon.

C.M. Yes, you do get props for that! *Q#8.* Do you have any pets? Again, we're just trying to get to know you.

S.J. Well, I love animals, but I can't take the chance of having a dog and losing clients who are allergic to dog hair. I do have a very sweet squirrel who lives in the tree out front, whom I spoil, and there is a dog who lives somewhere in the neighborhood who likes to spend his days lying in the sun on my front porch.

C.M. Almost done! *Q#9.* What do you picture yourself doing in five years?

S.J. Operating the best salon in the state, of course.

C.M. Good answer. And finally, *Q#10.* Any last words from you?

S.J. I'd like to invite everyone to just come see us once. I'm confident you'll come back, and you'll be happy with the work we do. Your readers can take a virtual tour to see the salon and meet the staff on our website:

SarahJoyConscilience@webnet.com.

~~~~~~~~~~~~~~~~~~~~~~~~~

The City Magazine thanks Sarah Joy from the newest salon in town, The Conscilience. We welcome her to the city, and wish her the best of luck. (I think it's time for a trim—I'm going to call her!—R. Formali, reporting.)

- 1b -

INTRODUCTIONS

Grace and William paged through the scrapbook, then strolled from room to room, casually looking at everything, like they were in a museum for the first time.

"I think I'm gonna enjoy this," William said.

"It really is a special place," Grace said, "for everyone who knows her. It's no surprise Sarah Joy has so many admirers. People just like to be with her, and she makes them all feel so special. I think if you picked ten of her clients and asked them to describe the salon, you'd get ten very different answers."

William looked puzzled. "Why's that?"

"She's a social chameleon. She's good at adjusting to the challenges she faces in everyone she meets," Grace started to explain. "Even I can't make an appointment for someone. Did you know that?"

"Why?" William asked. "How hard is it? You look in the book, tell the person when some openings are, and they pick one, right?"

"Oh, no, no, no, no, you silly boy," Grace smiled. "I don't know how myself. There are a lot of considerations. Probably you have to use differential equations at some point, I'm not sure." Grace laughed. "As far as I can tell, the day is divided into mornings, afternoons, and evening specials. In the mornings, many of our older clients come in. They feel totally at home with other senior citizens around. Even if you're the first gray hair here, you feel at home. Your fur coat will be hung on a silky hanger in the coat closet. Did you notice there's one hanging in there now? It's there just to keep others company. You're always at home here, even when you're the only client!"

William smiled. "I did notice that there seemed like a lot of gray hairs here in the mornings. And you're right: some of them did wear fur coats. I had no idea!"

"Well, William," Grace said, "just because you don't hang with women who wear dead animals, it doesn't mean they're not around. Just like nuns—you never seem to see them in public anymore, but you know they must exist."

William had to smile at that one. Grace's smile quickly turned to a look of concern. "However, young man, I'd suggest you get this 'old lady hat' and 'gray hairs' stuff out of your system. Sarah Joy will come down on you hard."

William started to protest—it was Grace who first mentioned "gray hairs"! But best to let it drop, he decided.

"Thanks for the warning!" William said. "Maybe we should come up with a code word or something."

"For old ladies?" Grace asked. "Hmm. Why don't we call them 'Helens'? Yes, that would work. If there is an elderly lady at the counter and I don't see her, you can just tell me that Helen needs me."

"Code words! This is so funny. I'm like a beauty parlor secret agent," William laughed.

Grace scowled again.

"I'm guessing 'beauty parlor' is out too. Fine." William rolled his eyes.

"Anyway," Grace continued, "younger clients tend to come in during lunch and after work. Stay-at-home parents, whom you would probably call 'housewives'— inappropriately—take up much of the afternoons, getting their hair and their kids' hair cut. If there's a mix of Helens and younger people for a morning, one set may be scheduled into my salon, and one set into Sarah Joy's. It's all about making people feel comfortable, like they fit in. It's sweet to watch how hard she works sometimes, even though many of the clients probably wouldn't care. Still, some scheduling details are interesting. Many of the old ... uh ... Helens really don't like little screamers around, but one, Mrs. Martin, just adores the Jackson twins, so Sarah Joy often finds a way to schedule them both in at the same time. I'll tell you, these kids have brought Mrs. Martin back to life! They've become her new family!"

William smiled. "I answered the phone once and the caller said they wanted to be scheduled in for the next Saturday night. Was that code for something?"

"'Saturday night,'" Grace repeated. "It's like the end of the day on Saturday. I would have thought you'd heard of it."

"Ha, ha," William deadpanned. "Just tell me!"

"On some Saturday nights, The Conscilience is open for business by appointment only. Regulars are scheduled in, often as couples. Friends may be scheduled in adjacent time slots. They show up with wine and cheese (and a lot of food from Sarah Joy) and settle in for an evening," Grace explained. "Usually there are four lucky clients— handpicked, of course. They get haircuts while the others hang out and talk. So it's a working night for Sarah Joy, and an opportunity to really bond with her best admirers."

"Four people plus Sarah Joy," William said. "Where do they go?"

"Sarah Joy's salon, of course!" Grace said. "Sarah Joy is cutting hair, so she stands. There's always someone in the chair. She rolls in a few office chairs from the back room, and she always pulls out a foot rest or two from their hiding place in the coat closet."

"I should have known the office chairs were here for a reason," William said. "Not the most comfy thing I could think of, but at least they're easy to store."

"People just got used to them," Grace explained. "I think they sorta enjoy rolling around in them."

"Chair races?" William asked.

"That's a good idea," Grace said. "To be honest, I don't know. I've never been to a Saturday Night."

"Well, that's something we need to take care of," William said.

"Take your time, big boy," Grace smiled. "Everything is done for a reason here. We may not know it, but *she* does."

Changing the subject (again), William said, "So there's a few things I'm curious about."

"Shoot!" Grace smiled.

"What's with the, uh ... you know, when Sarah Joy talks, sometimes she stops and ... uh," William struggled for the right word.

"Ah, the 'Sarah Joy Pause,'" Grace said. "I should have explained that to you."

"I mean, is it real, or something she just does, like a little secret weapon?" William asked.

"I've heard her use it so well. Often she just wants a little more information out of someone, so she just stops talking, and sure enough, they'll feel uncomfortable at the silence and talk some more. She can be very effective in getting people to say things they have no intention of saying. Everyone spends time in the Sarah Joy Pause confessional—except for Sarah Joy, of course."

Grace paused, trying not to be too obvious. She didn't look at William. William said nothing. Time passed. Grass grew. Seasons passed.

"OK, OK," William said. "I give."

Grace looked at the wall and snorted. Working with William is going to be fun, she decided.

"OK, what else?" Grace asked.

"Upstairs. What's the story?" William asked.

"What do you mean? You know she lives up there, don't you?" Grace replied.

"Yeah," William said. "Have you ever been up there?"

"No," Grace admitted. "It's not my home, not my business."

"Does it ever look like Sarah Joy sorta floats when she walks?" William asked.

Grace laughed. "Yeah. Why? Don't you? You're such a typical male, falling in love with her already. I do think she sorta tries to glide or something when she gets a chance. Maybe it's the long skirts she likes to wear."

"Well, you wear them too," William pointed out. "Do you try to glide?"

"No, I'm not part of the weightless club," Grace said. "It is interesting that we both like to wear long skirts and longish dresses, though."

"OK, just for the record, I'm not in love with my boss," William was quick to squeeze in, not wanting the point to glide by. "Still, I have to confess ..."

Grace said nothing.

"Very funny," William said. "You don't have to pause it out of me. I'll say it. Sometimes in the morning I get here early to clean up, and I admit, I hang out right here, so I can watch her make a grand entrance down the stairs while I'm looking up at her. I'm sure she doesn't understand the impact on a guy when a woman glides down a flight of stairs—an elegant staircase in particular. I always feel like I should be telling her how great she looks and handing her a corsage. Then her parents should come out from nowhere. She would make me talk to them, and then they'd take our picture."

"God, a prom fantasy! You got it bad," Grace laughed.

"It's a guy thing. You wouldn't understand," William said.

"Another rule." Grace smiled. "When you talk, don't sound like a bumper sticker."

Grace laughed. William tried not to, but it was a funny line.

Grace suddenly got serious. "You know, there are lots of things for you to do around here, but Sarah Joy really is hoping to offer massages to her people. I know you do chair massages, and she bought that nice chair in the front room for you. She could use the extra income. Do you think it's gonna happen?"

"Well, no one has asked for a massage this week, as far as I know," William said.

"To be honest," Grace said, "I wasn't supportive of hiring a masseur. A lot of people in this area belong to the Athletic Club, and the club has people who do chair massages pretty much around the clock, without appointments."

William nodded.

"I've done this before, working part-time at two other salons in the area, so I know how to do a massage." William said. "Just let me offer some mini-massages to clients and see if I can slowly generate interest. Sure, the Athletic Club has some great people, but if you can come here and get a cut and a massage, and shop, that's an attraction."

"At the other places where you worked, who came in for your massages?" Grace asked.

"My clients have been mostly women," He smiled. "Working on women is fine, but some of them I can't help because they scream if I try and really work on a muscle that needs attention. In some ways, I most like working with men. They let me do my job, scream a little less, and it can be a great workout for me too!"

"Well, I'll mention it to all of my clients," Grace said. "We can make this happen. I'm confident. When you have time, there is one thing that *would* be really great for you to do for us."

"Anything," William said. "What should I do?"

"Skulk," Grace said.

"Skulk. Got it," William replied. "What are you talking about?"

"Just hang out, be around, listen, help to make the experience a magical one. When my client sits down, I usually ask them if they want anything to drink. I know Sarah Joy has you making coffee twice a day and stocking the fridge with soft drinks and juices. If you hear my client say they'd like to have a Pepsi, it's nice that I can treat them, but it's awkward for me to have to go get it. I want it to just appear here on the table beside them. Can you do that for us?"

"The skulking waiter," William said. "It will look strange on my résumé, but sure. Sounds like an interesting challenge! Not a problem."

"So are we all set for now? Will week two be easier for you now that we talked?" Grace asked.

"Definitely," William said. "This time together has been good. Thank you, Grace. I just have one last thing. Have you ever seen the magazine called *Healthy Images*?"

"The magazine for salon owners?" Grace asked. "Sure."

"Every issue highlights two salons. I think we should send them some things about The Conscilience to see if we can get Sarah Joy some national attention. The scrapbook is a great start. We can copy some of the clippings in there, write a cover letter, and maybe they'll consider writing an article about us!" William was seriously motivated on this one. "I can write a cover letter and you can edit it. The worst that can happen is that they say no. Are you with me?"

Grace looked at him, thought for a second, then high-fived him. Fortunately there was a copy machine in the basement. A pact was made not to tell anyone. A package was prepared and ready to be mailed before Sarah Joy walked back in through the door, arms empty, from her morning of shopping.

- 3 -

AN ACADEMIC SATURDAY NIGHT

One circle of clients whom you would never expect to get together is made up of Gary and his wife, Claudia, and Christian and his wife, Janet. Gary and Christian are both professors of engineering—one at the University, and one at a very good private college just a few miles from here. Although they essentially teach in the same town, they had never met until Sarah Joy brought them together. She assumed they'd appreciate knowing one another. Christian is a chemical engineer, while Gary is an agricultural engineer. They always *seem* to look forward to their next Saturday night, although Sarah Joy no longer shares the enthusiasm and has been making them less frequent participants.

Gary and Claudia are both sixty years old. Gary is six feet three inches tall; Claudia is five feet zero. Gary is a gentle guy and nice enough, always quick with a smile. He has one of those little chuckles that is used so often, sometimes you don't even know what it's for. He's had the same handlebar moustache since 1972.

Under his chuckling exterior, Gary is a man in a bad mood. When he was first recruited as a faculty member, it was an exciting time of expansion for the colleges and universities, and an exciting time in his career. He was the first to receive a major instrumentation grant from the National Science Foundation in the school of engineering at his college. Students competed for the opportunity to do graduate research in his lab. The first few years were great fun; then some students came in who were not of such high quality and didn't really want to do dedicated research, and Gary's enthusiasm started to wane. Three years later, his next research proposal was not funded. Within a few years, his research students graduated, his teaching load was increased, and raises were exceedingly small. At this point, new faculty hires were being offered more than Gary was being paid. That hurt! A part of his life slipped away, and he could not make the Herculean effort to get it back. In a few years, he'd gone from the hot young faculty member to a too-young has-been.

Even so, Gary smiles. You only wonder why until you meet his wife. Claudia has four distinguishing, memorable features: her hair, her dress, and her chest. Her hair is always a fine salt-and-pepper Jackie Kennedy. Her dresses—and she only wears dresses—are always soft, wool or Angora, and tight. Her boobs are, in a word, magnificent. Her dress always hugs them, individually and with care. They are always somehow "lifted and separated," and her flat belly gives her sixty-year-old chassis a shape to die for.

Much to the frustration of single men in the area, Gary and Claudia get along. They maintain a good life for themselves. One fact that everyone is aware of, but no one knows how they know, is that Claudia and Gary spend one week a year in Aruba at a nudist resort. They always come back glowing, very tan (from what they show us), and seemingly ready to get through another year, happy to be together. Claudia may have a job, but no one really knows. People are just happy to be in her presence and to look at her.

Christian and Janet are a separate matter. Both are forty-four years old. When Christian was hired at the University, the provost made a special effort to renovate

30

laboratory space and to fill the lab with instrumentation for him. Recruiting packages had changed from Gary's time to Christian's. When Christian came to the University, spousal/significant-other concerns were becoming an issue. They hired his soon-to-be-wife as part of the package to recruit him. Four kids later, Janet is, to her husband, a bitch. Unfortunately, their kids are occasionally so exceptional that neither will leave. Not to bore you with kid stories, but Christian and Janet's oldest son, Jason, who is ten, likes to work with metal. Some kids go to the store with their parents and beg for a skateboard. Jason begs for welding rod. Jason lives to create, lives to mix metals and shapes in new ways, and to experiment. On his tenth birthday, they gave him everything on his list: iron, steel, leather, files, and a dozen other pieces of raw material and tools. He made the most incredible sword for himself—a long, copper-clad blade with a blued steel edge.

When you meet them, Janet quickly establishes herself as frumpy and apparently in a rather bad mood, but she can be smart and interesting when you get her started. Christian is always entertaining, and can laugh enough for a room full of people. If only he were as good at listening.

When these four congregate, Claudia likes to bring cheese, so she always brings cheese. She likes to pick crackers that go with the cheese, and always finds unusual ones. They never come in a package, always in a baggie, so we don't know where she finds them or how many she's already eaten, but they are always unusually shaped and with tasty seeds on them. After a few confirming calls from Sarah Joy, Gary always agrees to buy the wine. He always chooses a French or German wine, and they're always mediocre. He's unaware that Argentina actually exports wine. Sarah Joy lets Gary buy the wine to provide an opportunity for the group to stroke his ego with praise.

Whenever Janet comes to The Conscilience, she brings cookies. Christian always brings nothing—just the observation that everything is already taken care of. So Sarah Joy bakes a few little things, gets some shrimp and dips, and some little desserts, so there will be food. Since this is not the first Saturday night for these four, they all know to arrive at five o'clock, plan on four haircuts completed by nine o'clock, with four fascinating hours of conversation and laughing and drinking and snacking.

This particular Saturday night, just to provide background entertainment, Christian and Janet were the first to show up—with their three-year-old.

You have watched parents who seem oblivious to the actions of their children, even when they run past you with a bloody knife. Christian and Janet are that couple. Throughout the conversation, Sarah Joy imagines their daughter Netta poking her sticky finger in outlets, sticking hairbrushes in her diaper, and licking hair off the floor. She disappears sometimes, then a clunk is heard, then she runs back in to the room. Usually, no one goes to see what she knocked down. She waits a few minutes to make sure there is no disciplining or questioning, then disappears again—back to work.

Tonight Sarah Joy jokingly announced, as she does every time, that she can't be a hostess; this is a work night for her, so "pour some wine, fill a plate, and relax. Have a seat or just roam around!" The polite made themselves at home; the oblivious tended to roam.

Janet was Sarah Joy's first head. The process is always a gradual one. Sarah Joy begins by massaging the neck and upper back and head—sometimes for a few seconds, sometimes for fifteen minutes. No one asks how she decides, because we might not want to know. Janet never asks for anything in particular. Tonight, as usual, Sarah Joy just cut off six weeks' worth of hair.

Gary asked Janet, who was already captive, if she'd like a plate of crackers and cheese, since Christian did not. Janet graciously accepted. With this four-plus-one, the girls usually talk together, and the guys then have to as well. Of course, it was only one guy until Christian eventually roamed back into Sarah Joy's styling room. Gary was forced to wait for him. Christian started in on one of his favorite topics, complaining about work, even though Gary knows he has nothing to complain about. Gary announced that there is to be no talk about work. This is a party! Christian rolled his eyes. *Party—right, Gary. With you here?* he thought.

You can tell that Sarah Joy is starting to panic about the fun rating for a Saturday night when she starts looking for things to talk about. Tonight she picked a random hat on the wall and told a little story about its former owner. Christian decided he was going to have to start having fun himself because no one was going to do it for him.

No one would have noticed that Janet's cut was over, but everyone noticed when Claudia's began. She danced over to the hair washing-chair. Sarah Joy tipped the chair back for the hair wash. Up they came. Netta came back into the room to see what the new sound was, realized that it was just Daddy's heart beating louder, and ran off again.

Sarah Joy caught herself looking at the shadow of Claudia's nipples and decided she needed to try harder. She looked around the room and saw Christian just staring and smiling. Sarah Joy quickly threw a smock over the twins and got Claudia into the styling chair just as Claudia asked, "Christian, all I know is that you're an engineer too. What kind of work do you do?"

Oh God, more talking about work, and from this braggart! Gary thought as he finished off his glass of German wine and went for another. When he came back, Christian told Gary he'd paid Claudia $5 to ask the question, and then he laughed. Gary didn't.

While Gary had been getting his refill, Christian had run out to the car and had come back in with a bag.

"Well, I have several areas that I work in, but one is just too hot, so I have to share it with you," Christian explained as he pulled an unlabeled bottle of red liquid out of his bag. "I even came prepared."

He had dozens of little taste-testing glasses, and he poured a little something for everyone.

"It's good," Christian giggled. "Blueberry brandy. I made it in the lab. It may be one of the best you'll ever have."

Gary, disgusted, looked out the window, so Christian put Gary's glass of goodness on the table next to him, where it remained.

Christian pulled a footrest in front of Claudia, while Janet pulled out her phone and Gary plotted ways to create an explosion to shut Christian up.

"Claudia," Christian said, "I figure that if I'm not having a good time, nobody around me will, so I try to always have a good time. I've done some silly things in my life, and this is definitely one of them. It's so strange what funding agencies get excited about. I got my group of graduate students together one night in the lab and told them that they were all going to devote the next two weeks of their time to me. They were all to stop their current projects and all do some writing for me. Proposals to the federal government were due in three weeks, and I wanted to submit a new one."

Christian got up and started pacing the room as he talked. "With them all sitting around the conference table on a Monday night, I set a cardboard box on the table and proceeded to unload bottle after bottle of brandy plus my collection of shot glasses. They each tasted every one and took notes. They were all drunk by the time the group was finished. Then I asked them a set of questions. What did you think of #4—which was a fine, legitimate brandy? Those who didn't like it were sent to another table with bottle #4, and told to learn what a fine brandy tastes like. The rest of the samples were fruit brandies, made with peaches, cherries, or apricots. I explained that there was a good market for this stuff, although some of it is very fruity and sweet. I wanted to know how they felt about the other seven, how they ranked them, and why. How did each taste or feel? How did they respond to the smell and the texture? As they talked, I introduced some descriptive terms and they caught right on, using them as well. I have liked brandy since I was a little kid in Norway, so I looked into stills for making it. I found one that was state-of-the-art—truly art bordering on science. It measured all sorts of variables at several locations within the still, all monitored with a computer. You could use the computer to control a 'run' or to monitor how things changed throughout a run—to scientifically evaluate an accepted brandy-making method. I saw it at an international engineering meeting and fell in love with it. I wanted it."

"He wanted it," Janet repeated. "It's all I heard about."

As Christian talked, Sarah Joy moved Claudia's hair around and made clippy sounds with her scissors. Claudia didn't really need a haircut.

Christian continued his monologue, looking at Claudia occasionally to make it clear that *she* had asked! "We should be able to make our own brandy, better than anyone, I told my students, and once we learn how, we'll—well, we'll be able to drink like this every Monday night! This was my goal, to make the best brandy I could, so I could drink it!"

On he went. "I took a few minutes making notes on what would appear in my proposal as a survey, to find out what people liked and didn't like about brandy. Surveys are good; you can use them to convince people of anything. I surveyed my drunks as to what kind of fruity brandy they liked. One of my students, Louis, laid his head down gently on the table and said no more. Ted, another one of my gang, pulled a trash can next to his chair, just in case. Then there was Rich—you know Rich, don't you, Gary?"

Gary was quick to answer on this one. "Yeah, he's one of your dopier graduate students. Your department will only let him get a master's degree while all the others are in the PhD program, right?"

Christian followed up. "Right, not the smartest guy on the block. But I don't believe it after that night. Rich stood up and walked around the table as he talked, much like a lawyer would, except that he stumbled several times, bumping into people's backs, making them spill their drinks, and generally pissing them off.

"'And so we are at a delicate turning point,' Rich dramatically said to them. 'We sit at a fork in the road that will either give us good brandy or make us rich.' With this line, I sat up, and decided not to tell Rich to sit the fuck down."

"'You know what will happen?' he asked his fellow grad students. 'We'll all graduate and Christian will keep drinking. Do you think he'll send us all bottles of hooch for the rest of our lives? I think not. So let's think of getting rich. We need to figure out how to make a great, international-quality brandy, and patent the process. I want each of you to do a little drunk driving; get out there and each bring back a blueberry brandy or a blueberry wine. Liqueur stores are still open. Let's move, people!'

"So suddenly Rich is running my group!" Christian laughed. "He just took charge. They all got up and stumbled out, no questions asked. A few minutes later they all stumbled back in looking for car keys, then stumbled out again, no questions asked.

"'Does this always happen when you drink?' I asked Rich. 'What are you thinking?'

"Rich said, 'Well, I was reading about all of the antioxidants in blueberries, so I thought we could market blueberry brandy as something good for people, and excellent brandy as well. The first patented brandy, and expensive!'

"Rich had no clue how great this idea was. We had just had 'Ag Explosion' on campus, an annual meeting for farmers and suppliers, which I always go to because I always meet interesting people, see some new things, and collect free cups and key chains and stuff. The state blueberry growers were out in full force. They do a good job and, as an organization, they have money, but they just don't know what to do next. We grow great blueberries here. The season is just a bit short, so they naturally grow thicker skins, to protect themselves when the weather gets colder, which leads to a much tastier product. If we developed something using only blueberries grown in our state, they would absolutely love us!

"So as the others staggered in, Rich was telling me why he sent a bunch of drunks out on the road. He explained that he knew that brandy wasn't cheap, but it was a perfect time to do some more taste testing, so he wanted each guy to buy one bottle while they were drunk, because they wouldn't spend that much when they were sober! The kid's a genius, Gary, I swear."

"Sounds like another con man—a chip off the old block in your lab, right?" Gary said.

"Damn right!" Christian agreed.

Christian refilled everyone's drinks except Gary's, because he was pouting. Even Sarah Joy had some, and she never drinks while she's working! Christian continued, enjoying his fourth shot. "In the next two weeks, I wrote a mediocre proposal requesting money for my fancy new dream still and funds for training graduate students in the art of making the best blueberry brandy in the world, explaining how they could find a way to make it better than the best brandy—a German cherry brandy called *'Kammer Kirschwasser.'* I called the state Blueberry Growers Association and told them what I was doing. What the heck, maybe they'd write a nice little note to the governor! But no! They invited themselves in the next day and listened to a hastily prepared pitch on the new 'product.' They offered to 'chip in' $100K a year for three years to support the rapid development of the product, for a 50 percent share of sales—if it got to that—or a promise to only use blueberries bought in-state. Overnight, I ordered my dream still using their money! I modified the proposal, to indicate that the Blueberry Growers Association had already provided part of the funds for this ambitious project (which now required a *second* still, I decided). The National Science Foundation proposal reviewers praised the proposal as an example of universities and state business people working together to make new products, create jobs, and even to create a healthier planet—like this stuff would be the antioxidant elixir that would keep us young and cancer free! I asked the NSF for $300,000 and got $450,000. Unheard of."

Christian laughed and laughed. Fame, success in science—it all just fell in his lap. Gary would have sold his soul for that kind of attention, but he couldn't get close. It pissed Gary off. The only thing that made him relax was watching Christian's occasional glance at Gary's wife's boobs. *You can't* always *get what you want, big shot,* Gary thought. He hoped he was right.

Everyone else thought the story was a great one, and they were actually enjoying the Christian show! As Sarah Joy switched from Claudia's hair to Christian's, he continued to fill in some details on international sales of brandy, and how they had used some of the federal funds to convert part of the lab into a bit of a taste-testing lab, with a circle of leather Barcaloungers, each with a laptop, so students and guests could record their responses to the experimental products of the week.

So Christian's proposal had been funded, and he did the work as promised. He found that, using the traditional methods of making brandy, there were a number of not-so-desirable components that distilled over in the middle of the "run," so he diverted them out, making a very pure, luxurious, and healthy brandy. He bought four stills, bottled four hundred bottles by himself, distributed them at a few national and international brewers' conventions, patented his approach, and had now been bought out by a well-known American beer brewer who had decided they were going to get into the distilling business. Janet had helped design labels for the four hundred bottles that he gave away, using some pictures of the campus in the background. Christian got—well, let's say he got more than a million for full rights to the patent (shared among him, the state blueberry growers, his current students, and the University).

Gary would never have discussed money like that in public. He would sooner hang himself!

As Gary became Sarah Joy's final victim of the night, a very satisfied Christian laid down on the floor, since the room was spinning just a little too fast at the moment. Gary made a point of stepping over him as he went to sit in the styling chair.

Early in the conversation, Claudia had kiddingly referred to Gary as "Handlebar." Gary had said that sometime he'd like to talk to Sarah Joy about changing his look. His wife's eyes lit up, not unseen by Sarah Joy, and now a razor moved with lightning speed from trimming the back of his neck to his cheek. Bzzzz! Off came half his moustache. Gary was speechless. It had been a part of him for so long!

Sarah Joy said, "Sometimes you just gotta hold your breath and do it!"

"You look great, Gary," she said as she swiped off the other side.

Gary didn't seem to recall being told to hold his breath. Not that this was life and death—it was just a little hair. He looked much younger, and everyone approved. However, Gary does not move so fast, and cannot deal well with changes. His only choice was to sulk. Pouting and sulking—the perfect combo.

With Christian on the floor, talked out, Sarah Joy almost contemplated picking another hat to discuss, but just couldn't do it. She prayed to Bon Jovi, the god of hair, for help. *Help me, Bon Jovi: I need some excitement here!*

Suddenly the front door practically blew open. The hinges whined, like Richie Sambora bending a high note on his Fender Stratocaster to signal that the prayer had been answered.

"Who's there?" Sarah Joy politely asked.

"Lesbians!" was the giddy reply.

Sarah Joy laughed. Jan and Deena from next door breezed in and took over. The girls weren't ready for haircuts, but they had seen that the lights were on and thought they'd stop by. Jan, who runs a fairly big office at the University, is a beautiful African-American woman who, after being married for many years and having generated two sons, decided she was gay. Were it not for Sarah Joy, Jan would have boring hair. Fortunately, Sarah Joy "can handle black hair like a colored girl" (Jan's words), and is always ready to do braids or extensions. Deena swears that Sarah Joy is a black woman in a skinny white woman's body. Deena is, as you may guess, the wild one of the pair. She's a steam train, baby, riding down your track. She is a skinny little sweetie, with cherry Jello-dyed hair. Jan and Deena obviously are in considerable love with each other—they can never be found when they're not touching somehow, unless they're at work.

Sarah Joy loves having the lesbians over, and always squeals, "Sweet! Lesbians!" when they arrive. Jan and Deena love the response and like to use it wherever they go.

Gary sighed as they pranced around the room giving everyone little kisses. Deena even climbed on top of

Christian, still on the floor, and faux-grinded on him as he got his little kiss.

Now none of the four partiers had met Jan and Deena before, but when a cutie freight train comes through, the last thing you do is complain—you just enjoy the experience, if you're smart.

Christian thoroughly loved them because they increased the number of people watching Claudia's clingy dress. The only difference is, whenever Claudia jiggled a little (or God help us, bent over), Christian would smile but Deena would let out a little moan of approval. Gary decided if there was one more boob bounce accompanied by a moan, they were leaving. Janet just wished she had her camera to document the event.

The Lesbians filled Sarah Joy in on their most recent adventures, again invited her for dinner, filled Gary's appointment time very well with conversation, then decided they had to go because *American Idol* was coming on. They resisted the urge to leave in a flurry of kisses, because both *wanted* to give Claudia a full French kiss with a little squeeze, so they just had to be good, for Sarah Joy's sake, and do nothing. Sarah Joy smiled the whole way through their visit, just happy to know them and to watch them enjoying their lives. Throwing kisses at everyone, they pranced toward the door.

"Oh, what's this?" Deena said as she made a u-turn, spotting Gary's full glass of something. She downed it in a millisecond, did another "mmmmm," left the room, then ran back in to empty all of the other glasses. Considering that as the best compliment of the night, Christian told her to take the bottle of his brandy, which she eagerly did.

With Gary's trim over, they all decided to call it a night. Even though Sarah Joy felt it was a good night, she might not get these two couples together again for awhile, but in the end, everyone left laughing—well, laughing until they stepped out of the styling room.

Netta was asleep on the rug. Aveda products were falling out of her pockets and her lips were red. Netta vomit covered much of the rug. The rug, which had been special ordered, was shaped like a hat, and was a very tasteful purple. Gary looked at the puke and wondered what kind of three year old eats shrimp and feta cheese. It was discoloring the rug at lightning speed. Sarah Joy speed-meditated, working hard to not react. Gary and Claudia would have understood if Sarah Joy had just rolled up the rug with Netta in it and planted her in the back yard. Christian and Janet turned Netta upside down, shaking everything out of her pockets—all of which just fell onto/into the rug. Not thinking to offer any assistance in cleaning up, Christian was the first out the door, with Netta drooped over his shoulder. Bubbles came out of her mouth, which Janet wiped off with her hand. She thought they smelled like shampoo, and shrugged. Sarah Joy didn't even bother to survey the damage in the salon; she just turned out the lights and went upstairs to bed. Tomorrow, with some sleep and renewed strength, she'd be prepared to begin to take on the Netta aftermath.

No one really understood that Christian's story of accidental success so seriously bothered Gary, but it did. After the party, Gary dropped Claudia off at home, offering to run to the store for some ice cream, but instead he went into the University. He had taught there one summer, and still had some keys. He used his key to open a door to open a key box to open a door to find a key that opened Christian's lab. He knew the system there well. Once inside, he started picking up bottles that were all over the lab. What a mess—what an alcoholic mess. He grabbed an impressive, expensive-looking bottle, wound up nicely, as though he were on a pitcher's mound, and threw the bottle against the wall. It shattered for him. Nice pitch! He wished he'd had a batter. Picturing the place covered with sticky broken glass, he decided that he could do better. He took a half-empty bottle over to the sink, filled it to the brim with water, and shook it. He did this with all the bottles, knowing that once these clowns saw that their liqueur had been messed with, they'd have to throw it all away. Gary could think of nothing that would hurt them more than to have to pour their own alcohol down the drain.

As he was finishing up, a student stopped by to pick up a notebook he'd left behind in the lab. He and Gary briefly looked at each other. This student was in the summer class that Gary had taught there, an introductory engineering course, so they knew each other. When questions began the next day, the student said he saw someone in the lab but didn't recognize him. Of course he didn't—the man had no big moustache!

Gary smiled as he filled the last bottle, but he was not content. "More to come, you clowns," he said darkly as he locked up and went home. "More to come."

Fortunately for Christian, Gary tends to be a big talker, particularly when he's drunk and talking to himself.

- 4 -

THE JOY OF FORENSICS

Four massive columns rose three stories above the thirty-six marble steps that Sarah Joy climbed. Across the front side of the fourth floor, above the columns, foot-high capital letters spelled out "STATE POLICE" in gold. Sarah Joy wanted to do the Rocky-Philadelphia-Art-Museum-Steps dance—she was so excited. She also wanted to run back to her car and never keep her appointment.

Milicia "Millie" Hilcock watched from her second-floor lab window as Sarah Joy climbed the front steps. They had only spoken on the phone, but Sarah Joy was easy to spot. Not many people come into the lab at 10:30 AM unless it's for a meeting or they're in a body bag. When Millie was hired, she thought she could do the job. She now knew she could not. It's the kind of work you can't learn at school; you need to be trained by someone with experience. There was no one here to help her when she arrived, no high-level person ready to teach her. Embarrassed, she struggled to do the best she could. She finally admitted that she needed help. Lt. Zalombe, her supervisor, reluctantly agreed to let her hire a consultant on a limited basis.

"We're not made of money, you know," he told her as he signed the contract. Millie had started her search by doing some research on wig manufacturers, identifying the premiere company, and trying to talk to some of the experts in wig design. They pointed her to some tutorial websites and a few useful books, but they had no provisions for either training or providing staff as consultants. They offered to do a zip-code search to identify their biggest clients in the area. Sarah Joy popped up at the top of their list. The second on the list was a salon called Donald K's on 58th Street. She contacted the Donald and told them she was looking for someone with hair and facial reconstruction experience, and they had one suggestion—again, a former employee of theirs, Sarah Joy. A good conversation on the phone between Millie and Sarah Joy—and Sarah Joy's willingness to jump right in—sealed the deal.

Sarah Joy tried hard to look like she knew what she was doing as she scoured the first floor for a list of inhabitants and office numbers, then headed for the elevator. A few minutes later, a frustrated Sarah Joy turned the fourteenth corner of the marble-walled hallways—all of which were lined with identical black doors and frosted glass panels—and decided to take the stairs. But her heels were a little too high and a little too unworn to make stairs simple, which made the locked door on the second floor—and the third floor, and the first floor— even more frustrating. Locked in a stairwell—what a place to die. Well, at least when they found her cell phone on her car seat, they'd know to come looking for her.

The first bead of sweat made Sarah Joy realize that stairwells aren't usually air-conditioned. "Well, perhaps this is where I should begin to panic," Sarah Joy said aloud. She tugged on the first-floor door through which she had begun this adventure. She pushed, pulled, even started to bang on it. No one was rescuing her.

Now Sarah Joy knew that this was not the end. Somehow she would get out. Still, spending a day in a stairwell is an embarrassing way to miss an appointment.

There was an asymmetry to the landings for each floor. The second floor had a second, unmarked door. In a mild panic, Sarah Joy charged the door, twisting the knob as her shoulder slammed against the chipping red paint on the heavy metal door. As it opened, it was instantly clear why the doorknob was warmer than the others. Sarah Joy, moving faster than she realized, was suddenly across the threshold and outside in the sun. Ten officers with raised weapons aimed and prepared to fire. Suddenly a shot rang out. Six officers ran toward her at the far end, the target end, of the shooting range. No one was amused; no one was even very interested in knowing how she got there. At position four, Lt. Zalombe removed his ear protection, locked and packed his pistol, and collected his thoughts as he collected her information and escorted her to Millie's office.

"Welcome to the State Police Forensics Laboratory, ma'am," he said. "Please confine your guest to this laboratory, Millie." And that was all he had to say, for now.

Our two deer-in-the-headlights just stood and stared at each other. Millie was a fair-skinned thirty-something, the no-nonsense kind of person you'd expect to find in a police role. Her straight black hair was so thick that her haircut resembled a helmet. The jeans and the shirt tied above the waist surely irritated the officers, as non-uniformed civilian employees usually do.

Millie, conscious of the time, kept small talk to a minimum and got straight to the point.

"Sarah Joy, you come highly recommended as someone with lots of wig experience, and you know that I offered to hire you for one week as a wig and hair consultant. You know we're at the State Police Crime Lab, and I feel very

49

bad that I hid information from you when we talked, but I need your help. Hopefully, you've anticipated this, but maybe not, so I'll just ask: do you think you can work with dead people?"

Sarah Joy sat on the lab stool and smiled. Millie took Sarah Joy's calmness as a yes.

"What I do is important work. People benefit from it. Please, just let me show you what I do," Millie said.

"Millie, it's OK." Sarah Joy turned on her warmest smile. "I have worked with dead people, and I do have some idea of what you do. Just show me what you need."

Sarah Joy tried her best to act as though the combination of smells—formaldehyde and wet clay—was a commonplace thing for her as she entered the lab.

Millie started her tour of Millie. Working full tilt, she can do fifteen to twenty people per year. That's a rough head count. As the details unfolded, she slowly led Sarah Joy past the first lab bench, around the corner, and into the back half of the lab. Here, all of the lab benches had been removed, leaving a large, open area with lots of lights and a small table in the center. To one side was a pile of paper-wrapped packs of clay, drawers of glass eyes, and a counter strewn with lipstick, makeup, and brushes.

On Millie's wall was a picture of a bearded man, unidentified. The man was Alexis Hurdli Ka, who immigrated to the US from Pakistan in 1881, before Pakistan even existed, and who became a national treasure because of his knowledge and creativity in analyzing evidence to determine whether remains were of human origin, and if so, the age at death, sex, stature, ancestry, and evidence of foul play. His work led to an entire field of forensic science. He was Millie's hero.

To the rear was a wall covered with paper—sketches of faces and photos, pinned up everywhere. A glance at the desk made Sarah Joy cringe (as did her Apple stock) when she saw the hopelessly outdated PC.

On the table was a head. No dead body, no corpse. A head. "Disembodied" had long been one of Millie's most favorite words, even before the lab was part of her life. Her grandmother, religious zealot of the Hilcock family, took great pride in two of what she considered to be religious *objets d'art*. The first was a six-foot high copy of a painting of a bewilderingly tall Jesus knocking on the UN building like it was someone's front door. The second item was a twelve-inch-high glass sculpture of "praying hands" that could be lit from a light bulb within. The first left Millie amused. She referred to it as "Big Mother Jesus." The second she took great joy in calling "The Disembodied Hands."

"Grandma, this is gruesome. Two hands cut off a body, pressed together. How can you condone such a crime?" she'd harass her grandmother.

"Oh, dear God, child, they are praying hands—praying to the Almighty. This is art, my dear—and one of the most common images of the Christian faith."

"Grams, it ain't art if it says 'made in Thailand' on the bottom. If this is what they do to you when you pray, I'll pass. How can you embrace a faith that adores disembodied body parts?"

And so their relationship went. When Grams died, as per her explicit wishes, she lay in her coffin, old and angelic, with her hands sitting atop her waistline—ever so tastefully wired together. Millie had mixed feelings—she still wanted to harass her grandmother over the choice, but technically they were not disembodied; creepy, but not disembodied.

Millie was classified as an AO-05–grade artist on the state payroll. Usually Millie was not involved in homicides and suicides in this part of the state—unless there were extreme head-related trauma aspects of the case, such as disembodied heads or badly damaged heads, frequently hanging by a thread. In some cases, there was not much head at all. For some badly decomposed remains, "head" meant "skull." Millie's job was to reconstruct the head—usually not for burial purposes, but to assist in identifying a dead soul. Millie is extremely dedicated, and her work has led to the identification of a few victims—but mostly not. Few understood that this was a common outcome.

Sarah Joy had seen a primer on the process of facial reconstruction on the Discovery Channel one sleepless night at 1 AM—scientists were taking cavemen's skulls and attempting to rebuild the faces. Millie explained the process of determining the amount of flesh likely on different parts of the skull, based on body size, diet, clothes, anything. Then, a thin layer of clay over thousands of precisely placed clay plugs makes the face begin to take shape. It all seemed very familiar to Sarah Joy.

"You must be a great sculptor, Millie," Sarah Joy said.

"I had the best letter of recommendation from my mentor because I have no artistic talent. Others in the field are very talented in creating expressive faces. I do nothing. I inject no artistic aspect at all. I create an unbiased face that is most often ID'd by a family—actually recognized by someone. Everyone else makes faces that look like Elvis or Queen Latifah.

"Let me introduce you to Bobette 4 here. All the males are Bobs, and all the females, Bobettes. Her head was slashed seventeen times with a machete before it was completely removed from her neck. I have photos of some parts of her face. I know her lips were full. I know how her eyebrows looked. I have to build a reasonable copy of her head to get pictures out to try and get her identified. But Sarah Joy, I never did full heads. We'd always just plop a wig on at the end. I need to do the hair, not just the face, and make it look both natural and neutral."

And so Sarah Joy's consulting job began. She and Millie stayed until midnight on the first day, inventing for themselves ways to secure hair, blending hair into clay hairlines. Sarah Joy even experimented in making stubby eyebrow hairs at one point, using cut-up brush parts, before her day was done. Bobette 4 had become important to them both. Maybe it was because her all-Gap wardrobe confirmed that she was probably no more than eighteen. Millie and Sarah Joy shared the passion needed to get the girl identified.

By week's end, the head was done (but, four weeks later, it still hadn't been identified). Millie and Sarah Joy enjoyed each other, and neither of them had been looking forward to week's end. Sarah Joy promised to sneak back in periodically to help, gratis. More than once, Lt. Zalombe noticed Sarah Joy's car in the lot, especially when he was leaving for the day. While he never stated it aloud, he had much respect for both women.

- 5 -

A VISITOR ARRIVES

"Hi, I'm Sarah Joy," she said, her warm hand extended through the front door, as a cool autumn wind blew in. Warm hand, genuine warm smile—something every customer looks forward to. To keep warm, Sarah Joy was wearing the every-color sweater that her mother had made for her. Her full, flowered skirt billowed in the breeze. A friendly welcome seemed somehow insufficient for the visitor, who, untouched by a warm smile or a cool wind, climbed the last step and walked past her 9:00 AM appointment.

"Diane, Diane Grim," the visitor said. A second chill blew in. It always happens when she says her full name.

Diane Grim is the assistant to the editor of the magazine *Healthy Images*. In each issue, a few salons are highlighted from around the country. Sarah was never told how they learned of The Conscilience, but she had been informed last week that Ms. Grim was being sent to collect information for an article.

"Possible article" is the phrase that Diane was quick to use. Grim was tall and flawless. Her plum wool jacket matched her short wool skirt—the publisher's uniform. A gold chain with a single white pearl sat on her chest. The white silk blouse was also standard issue. When you looked at her cleavage (and you did look at her cleavage), it was never clear whether the blouse was low-cut, or if she was just well-endowed. This was the look that the company required. Impeccable hair, in every way, was of course, assumed. Flawless skin, in every way, was of course, assumed. She didn't get to where she was without exceeding all expectations.

Diane did not seem to enjoy the prospect of smiling. Perhaps it had never occurred to her to try it. Sarah Joy had never stopped smiling since she was born, when she offered a warm hand to the waiting nurse and doctor.

Not in any great rush to participate in a conversation, Diane took in the shop. She slowly, deliberately, and somewhat dramatically turned her head, and only her head, to survey the brightly lit front room, shimmering with Aveda products. For her, this did not seem to be a delightful surprise, but an expectation. She walked from end to end, looking each section of wall up and down, like a general looking over the troops.

She stopped. "How can you not stock ..." she started to ask. Then she just shook her head and walked away, mid-inspection. Her eyes and accompanying head moved back to the center of the room, to the stairs leading to the second floor. Diane was not the first to wonder what the upstairs held, but she seemed to be driven by a unique sense of contrary purpose. She needed to be in charge. After all, she was. She could decide if a salon was to become nationally known or not. For someone only twenty-eight, she was either very impressed with her own power, or just a jerk. She held her scanning head high.

"Well, let's sit down and talk, shall we?" she asked, looking out the window. She could have been talking to the squirrel, who preferred to sit in the tree rather than be indoors with Ms. Grim. This was not the first squirrel to hold that opinion.

As Diane spoke, she moved toward the stairs, trying to make the movement seem natural, as if she had been

56

invited to go upstairs—as if upstairs was where they *should* sit and talk; as if upstairs was the right place to be, the only place to be, the place where she could decide to hold this interview.

Sarah Joy smiled, took a slight lead, and moved into her styling room. Diane scowled, having no choice but to follow.

The silence of swords being sharpened swelled around them. The room, of course, had only two permanent chairs, one for washing, one for styling.

"Have a seat," Sarah Joy said cheerily, pointing toward the styling chair. "I talk to people best when they are comfortable and I'm standing—usually behind them."

"Well, if you'd like to go upstairs, that would certainly ..." Diane attempted one last time.

Sarah Joy cut her off in mid-sentence. "No, I live upstairs and your visit is about my salon, so you should see what I have down here." A sword sliced through the thickening air.

William walked through, balancing six boxes of gloves. A simple "hi" from him stimulated no response from Diane, so Sarah Joy passed on making introductions. *Let her wonder who these people are as they walk through*, she thought.

Everyone was now in place—Diane in the chair, swiveling, looking at herself in the full-wall mirror before her, and Sarah Joy standing by the entryway to the room.

She kept a constant eye on Diane, using Sarah Joy Vision: Follow the reflection from the window glass to the wall mirror to the face of the person in the chair. She knew every reflection, every double reflection, that would allow her to keep an eye on someone's face, no matter which way either of them were facing. Home turf.

"Well, I usually don't ask many questions of those we interview. I just let them hang themselves." Diane waited too long before she (literally) cracked a smile, as if the comment was supposed to be funny.

"What we usually do is give someone an opportunity to tell us about their salon," she continued, "how they personally make it unique, how product selection makes it unique, and of course readers like to get to know a salon owner. So, I can take some notes and you can just start telling me the story of this ... place."

Sarah Joy handed her a business card. "The Conscilience. This place is called The Conscilience. You know ... William Whewell?" Sarah Joy told herself to stop being so catty, and took a deep breath to try and do a start-over.

"Of course," Diane said flatly. "If there *is* a story, we'll arrange to have the photography staff come in later. But we don't need to go through those details quite yet. I must admit the interior is striking. The rooms are really very beautiful. You should be commended." (Not that Sarah Joy *was*, in fact, being commended—just that she should be.)

"Thank you," Sarah Joy said politely. She had to again make a personal commitment to a good visit. "Would you like something to drink? I have coffee on, Eight O'Clock, the only coffee we serve; and we do have water and soft drinks."

Diane looked her in the eye for the first time, and asked, "Do you have Fresca?"

"I'm very sorry, no. But I do have Sprite," Sarah Joy replied.

(Pause.)

(No response.)

"Or some juices that you might be interested in."

Sarah Joy had failed a test.

"No, I'm fine," Diane said, as if she were a teacher who was pleased to write a red "F" on the test of the student whom she had never liked.

Fresca. Do they still make Fresca? Who in hell stocks Fresca? Who drinks Fresca? Could you have picked a more obscure soft drink? Perhaps a Lemon Pepsi Light? A Kona Pepsi? They've come and gone a decade ago. Surely that's your drink of choice, you nasty thing, Sarah Joy did not say while not shaking Diane until her hair looked mildly disheveled.

A pen and steno pad appeared. Sarah Joy raised an eyebrow. She was very aware of Diane's accessories—or rather, the lack of them. No purse, no briefcase—she didn't come with anything!

Where are her car keys? Sarah Joy wondered.

It was unclear where a pen and steno pad could have been, but now they were out in the open. And what does Diane carry with her? How does Diane project her needless stuffiness and strange version of professionalism? With a plastic pen that says "Ace Hardware."

It was good to see a flaw so early in the visit.

Oblivious to the pen *faux pas*, Diane dove right in. "So, just for my own understanding, is 'Sarah Joy' your real name, or just one that you use—a stage name, if you will?"

"It's my real name," Sarah Joy smiled. It was an I'm-surprised-you're-asking-me-this smile. She had no choice. Throwing scissors would have been ... fun, but impolite.

"It's just that I don't think I've ever encountered anyone with the last name of Joy," Diane explained.

And I never met a bitch named Grim, Sarah Joy thought.

Wondering how a story with more than four sentences would play with Diane, Sarah Joy explained: "My great-grandmother came to the United States through New York. Her name is on the great list of names at Ellis Island. In the rush of processing immigrants, someone only copied down her first and middle name. She had my grandfather with her, still a baby. When asked the child's name, she said Elliot, so they recorded it as Elliot Joy. Hoping not to get anyone angry or to do anything that might hold up the process, my great-grandmother remained silent, accepting her new last name and the new last name of her small family. We have a long line of strong women in our family, but she was not willing to sacrifice a name for a future."

Surprisingly, Diane had not dozed off, but only because she hadn't thought to. She was looking out the window, much too glazed-over to actually be focused on anything. The squirrel was trying his best to give her the finger, but finally decided that he didn't know exactly what that meant. Diane's pen remained capped, and her steno pad remained unopened. Still, it appeared that gears were grinding inside that Grim head. Situations were being pondered. Questions were being considered. Questions like, *How do I get out of here?*

Sarah Joy could see this, but her only choice was to be honest, to let Diane get to know her and her salon a bit, and if no one could find a story here, so be it. Surely the photos alone would have created a unique spread for this magazine. The purple alone ...

"Tell me about this place," Diane ordered.

"Well, I'm not sure where to begin. We only serve nice people." Sarah Joy folded her hands like a young (lying) child praying, designating simplicity and purity.

"Really?" Diane scowled. "How in the world does that work?" Her words were drawn out painfully, created only because she had a job to do, not because she wanted to know the answer.

"Well, I have a very nice staff, and all nice clients. They are authentically *nice* people," Sarah Joy said, not exactly answering the question. There was a good reason. It was a line that had just popped out, and Sarah Joy was totally unprepared to explain what she had just said. *"We only serve nice people"? Where in the world did that come from?* Sarah Joy didn't say while not lightly banging her forehead against the nearest purple wall.

"How do you get rid of the 'not nice' people?" Diane asked with a rather well-constructed dumbfounded look. She wanted to say, *What kind of horrible animal* are *you?* It would have been fun.

"Oh, did I say I got rid of customers? I'm sorry. That's not what I meant at all. Sometimes I just don't click with a person. Have you ever had that happen?"

(Pause.)

Sarah Joy didn't laugh so hard that she snorted. "Sometimes when that happens, they don't return. It just works out." Sarah Joy still had no idea where she was heading with this. What a stupid thing to say.

"So, you subtly make them feel unwelcome if you don't like them?" Diane pushed.

"Not at all. I know that it takes a while for people to get to know me, and I assume it takes a while for me to know them. Even my best, loveliest people have a bad and quiet day in here. I wouldn't discourage someone from returning based on one hour." Sarah Joy felt pretty good with that answer.

"So, it just *works out* that you have a pool of *nice people*?" Diane said. (Yet another person who spoke in italics.)

(Pause.)

Sarah Joy tried out a pause. She knows that it doesn't work on people who are oblivious to the pace and content of a conversation, but it seemed appropriate to launch another one in Diane's direction. Unfortunately, Diane was happy to just sit so that she could report an hour spent here. Whether she spoke or not was irrelevant, so the pause had no impact.

"I'm very fortunate, aren't I?" Sarah Joy finally said. "Do you work with any nice people?"

"Perhaps you can tell me about the physical shop," Diane requested. She had long ago decided that topics shift quickly in the interview business. "Most salons are not also homes, so you are obviously very involved. Are your home and work life fairly integrated?"

Sarah Joy looked at her, authentically perplexed. "What?"

Well sure, Sarah Joy didn't continue. *If I'm cutting the hair of a hot guy, or a sexy girl, it's just a short trip to the bedroom. This place rocks when Brian the FedEx guy shows up, and you have no idea how many toys I can order that are delivered by FedEx.*

Aloud she said, "Well, I probably don't have the most interesting home life at the moment. I just enjoy working, and right now my priority is making my business the best in the state. My staff has offered to get a neon light to put in the window that says, 'Always Open' because they think I work too much. We are open evenings until 8:00, and also Saturdays."

"Myyy, I guess that doesn't leave much time for a *per*sonal life." It wasn't a question; it was an observation from Diane. Sarah Joy left it unanswered.

And I guess being a bitch doesn't provide much opportunity for a per*sonal life,* Sarah Joy didn't reply.

"I'm still not getting much information, Sarah Joy. The building, the setup, the decor—tell me how it happened. Who did the decorating? Someone with national name recognition?" On this point, Diane was right: Sarah Joy was having a hard time focusing on the questions because Diane had so thrown her off.

"Well, I don't feel like I created it, but I tried to faithfully build what I saw when I first looked at the property. It was in bad shape, but I could see that it was once a beautiful home, and I thought that restoring it was something I had to do. It had potential, and I like potential. When I walked through the rooms, the only color there was brown, but I could see exactly how it would look—even down to where that chair would be that you're sitting in. I knew I would own it and I knew how it would look. I saw the colors, the floor plan, I just saw it. I created what I saw."

"To be honest, hon, I wouldn't tell people you looked into the future. Do you have these 'experiences' often? No, don't answer that. We'd never put such a story in our magazine. You never told me who did the work. You're not telling me you did it all yourself?" Diane asked.

All Sarah Joy had heard was "blah blah hon, blah blah blah." What nerve!

"I did a lot, like stripping off old wallpaper, but of course I had painters and some cabinet builders come in to do most of the work. Once they almost left me, but they were very patient. When they painted the walls up the staircase, the first big expanse of color, the purple just wasn't right. I described to them what I wanted, and they repainted. It just wasn't what it was supposed to be. The third time they painted it, they made it clear it was the last time. They were being paid by the hour, so I didn't see the problem, but I guess I was asking for more than they felt comfortable doing. Fortunately, they got it right the third time."

The sound of a cheap pen lightly tapping on the cardboard cover of a steno pad had the regularity, tone and volume of the kind of mantle clock that one would lovingly wind up daily—just the kind of clock that one might find at The Conscilience. Tap, tap, tap, tick, tick.

"I get the feeling you're not finding anything interesting here," Sarah Joy remarked.

"Perhaps I should try one last time to get you to focus … on the answers to some specific questions," Diane stated. "How did you get into the hair-care business? Let's try that." Diane finished the sentence with a sharp nod of the head, as if to make it clear that someone must take charge of this, and she would be the one to do it.

"Oh, my gosh, well, I certainly never *wanted* to be in the hair business." Even Sarah Joy rolled her eyes after she said *gosh*. "The summer after I graduated from high school in Minnesota, my parents gave me a choice. I could get a job or do nothing, and pay rent; go to school, and pay half rent; or become an adult, and move out. Well, I didn't want to pay them rent and I certainly didn't want to go to school. My friend, Mary, suggested that I go to the local beauty school. I had two friends named Mary; this is the other one. Anyway, we were driving around one day, and she stopped in front of the beauty school."

"'Why not check into it?' she asked.

"'Because I'm not interested,' I told her. She dared me. That didn't work. Then, in what was unusual for Mary, she constructed a logical argument.

"'Look,' she said, 'your parents could charge you something—let's say $200 per month. If you go to school, they'll only charge you $100 per month. If you go to beauty school, it might cost $100 per month. So, instead of giving your money to your parents, you'd get to go to school almost for free. How can you pass it up?'"

(As soon as she said it, even Sarah Joy wasn't sure the argument was a logical one.)

"On the second dare, I went in. There was a short, older woman who was in charge, one of a large number of short, older women who I encountered in this beauty school. As I was telling her about myself, looking through the blinds at Mary sitting in the car out front, the older woman suddenly became very animated, excused herself, and went off to see the owner, the one man in the building. They both came back very excited and interested in me. Apparently they offered a scholarship to my high school every year, but there were never any takers, and it got to the point where the high school declined it. A board member reportedly said that it might not be good to point any of the students in this direction, since they wouldn't make any money. Beauty schools have a bad reputation. But every salon owner started in one, and not all salon owners grew up in trailer parks. Anyway, the shorties offered me a scholarship on the spot. The only stipulation was that I would keep in contact for a three-year period after I completed their program, so they could collect data to prove that hairdressers make as much, if not more, as workers who have clerical and technical skills—proof to take back to the high school. So there I was, in beauty school!"

"Sarah Joy, why do you do this if you don't enjoy it?" Diane was actually curious to the answer to this question.

"Oh, Diane, I *love* what I do. I was such an unlikely choice for this school. I wasn't even interested in my own hair. Not like Mary—the other Mary. She was always playing with her hair, dying her hair, trying to do things with other people's hair. It drove me crazy. But once I was in beauty school, I had a great time. We learned a lot about the human body and anatomy, actually learned a lot of chemistry. I don't know much, but I love science. There were times during that year when I wanted to leave. I remember one day ... As students, we would go out to the waiting room, call the name of the next victim, bring them in, then discuss their hair with an instructor. One morning I went out for my first, called a name, got a very large woman. She wasn't the woman I called, but what did I know? I found the instructor and told her I had Mrs. Eggflap in the chair. She said, "Fine, just take care of her."

So I returned to the massive woman and asked what she wanted. Of course it was a perm, and with tight tiny curls. Do you know how small the smallest rollers are? Oh, of course you do. They are the size of pencils! So I started to roll, and roll, through lunch, no breaks, till 6:00 that evening. I still remember the feeling. She was so overweight that she had a fat, squishy head. That almost sent me running from this business, but you know what? There was a part that was very satisfying to me. I did something for someone and made them happy and feel pretty. That is what keeps me in this job."

"And that is Sarah Joy's story of becoming a salon owner," Diane deadpanned. "Pushed over the edge by a fat woman with a squishy head."

"Pretty much! One thing I should tell you is that I really did go to beauty school just because I was *not* going to pay my parents full rent. I got away with paying them $50/month. Little did I know that their plan all along was to put that money in the bank and give it back to me when I left home. They are sweet people, but had I known that, I probably wouldn't have gone to school at all."

"Well, this is all touching, but no one wants to know that their stylist started off despising her job," Diane said. At this point, Diane's remarks were becoming a lecture. "People want to believe that you've always wanted to do this, that this was the fulfillment of a dream."

"Well, in a way it was. If I didn't do this, I could see myself in some sort of health care, perhaps even working in a hospital or nursing home. Taking care of people is important to me, and I think I do it well." Sarah Joy was proud of this.

"Still, no one wants to hear the story of little Sarah Joy in beauty school. Usually, little is known of the best stylist's beginnings, only advanced training that they have recently received—did you study in Paris or New York perhaps?" Diane didn't wait for an answer. "I don't think your little story would make good text for our magazine."

"Well, I can't be who I'm not," Sarah Joy said. "Perhaps you should be talking to someone else—perhaps some of my clients. That would be a good idea, and maybe a new angle for you. Yes! Maybe they can best tell you what goes on here."

"I have a better idea," Diane said as she stood. "It's my opinion that you have a lovely shop, and you may well make good money and have lots of lovely, happy, and contented customers. But we need modern stories of modern people running state-of-the art facilities. Perhaps I can come back after you've had some time to think about *that*. If you can give me a good story, describing a vibrant and progressive owner, we'll consider putting something together. Maybe you just need some time to think about some less folksy stories about yourself, and less psychic stories of interior design. I should go now."

And with that, she was gone. She didn't even wait for Sarah Joy to walk out with her. It all happened so fast, but still, by the time she was out of the chair, her tools had vanished—returned to some unknown crevice from which they had been previously kept. One should have expected nothing more or less from Diane Grim.

And there Sarah Joy stood—standing perfectly still, left wondering what she should have done differently, wondering if losing Diane was a bad thing or a good thing. She said aloud to herself, "Well, good! I don't want to be in that magazine if you don't think my story is worth telling."

"Damn right!"

The two words echoed through the salon. The first was a celebration of Sarah Joy's comment, but by the second word, it was clear that the sentence wished it could have returned to its place or origin, unheard and undetected. William needed to stop sitting in the back room, listening to Sarah Joy's days. But once he started listening, he couldn't stop. Everything he heard reinforced the warm feeling he had: the happiness of working at The Conscilience—working for Sarah Joy. She smiled knowing that he was proud of her. That was worth much more than some stupid spread in some damn magazine.

Sarah Joy hoped she was right.

FYI, the next day, when a client was attending to her bill, she pulled a random pen out of a tasteful purple glass on the front counter to sign her credit card receipt. The pen said ...

Ace Hardware.

MERRY CHRISTMAS BABY

SARAH JOY
AND THE STAFF OF THE
CONSCILIENCE
REQUEST YOUR PRESENCE
AT OUR WINTER
WONDERLAND
SATURDAY, DECEMBER 23
2:00–5:00 PM.
COME CELEBRATE THE
HOLIDAYS WITH US.
COME HUNGRY.
COME THIRSTY (WINK!).
COME SHARE THE LOVE OF
THE SEASON,
MAKE NEW FRIENDS,
AND LET US THANK YOU
FOR BEING
LOYAL CLIENTS
AND FAMILY.

Every year Sarah Joy invites clients, neighbors, and people in her life to a Christmas party at The Conscilience. PC-related aspects of the word "Christmas" need not be rehashed here. It says "Winter Wonderland" on the invitation, but it's *her* Christmas party and she won't be bullied into calling it something else.

Sarah Joy budgets to create that warm and fuzzy feeling that many of those invited remember from their own Christmases past—it's her gift to everyone, and she takes the job seriously.

William had offered to come early to help in any way that he could, even to do the Santa thing. Sarah Joy smiled widely at the image of a short, Cuban Santa sneaking up on the guests. It sounded wonderful, but not this year.

"I just want you to come with the other guests, William," she said, and gave him a little hug. "This is your first Christmas here, so come and enjoy yourself, see how it works, meet people, and next year you can be more involved."

And so William arrived, trying to be fashionably late, with new slacks, a dress oxford shirt, paisley tie, and a very tasteful sweater vest. He'd been concerned over all the hype of the party when he left on Friday—nothing was being done! He hadn't noticed as he was pulling out of the driveway that a truck the size of a moving van was turning the corner.

William looked around. The salon has been transformed into a Christmas village. There were overstuffed chairs and sofas everywhere, creating little nooks and crannies where groups of varying numbers were settling in. A natural flow had been created from room to room, a path that guests could follow through the salon for those who preferred to cruise instead of sitting. With twelve decorated trees and four menorahs, at least eight distinct regions had been created. One would be just right for you.

William had decided that he would cruise, and Grace agreed that he could shadow her, or at least try, to help him learn about some of the guests.

Sarah Joy was now stuck with the line that says she only works with nice people, so William was curious to see if this was true. However, many of William's plans left his head as the smells, sounds, and feel of the season at its best welcomed him.

Sarah Joy floated over, gave him a Merry Christmas hug, and sent Grace upstairs with his coat. It was the perfect day for this party. Snow was falling! William wondered how she had arranged that. William was enjoying his hug when someone selfishly insisted on coming in behind him, and the next hug-ee had to be attended to.

William grabbed Grace as she came down the stairs.

"Grace, you look great!" he said, surprising himself. He took in her long Christmas skirt, her snowflake sweater that he wanted to crawl into because it looked so warm, and her festive red stockings. She contributed to the ambience of the party like a hippy elf. She was, of course, here to work, but as far as William was concerned, her assignment was to tell him who's who.

In an instant, Grace had accumulated some music CDs in one hand and a pile of small dirty plates in the other. She handed William the plates and took off on a mission.

Having no idea what to do with the dirty dishes, William stashed the plates behind the checkout counter. *If they're still there Monday morning, then I'll worry about them.* He realized that he was actually humming along with the background music that had just faded in, something he rarely did. The hum of the crowd was just right to give him permission, sour notes and all, and to ensure that only he heard his best Springsteen hum of "Merry Christmas Baby."

He grabbed Grace again as she flew by. "'Merry Christmas Baby'? You better be careful. I don't think the Helens think of this as Christmas music!"

"You're a Helen!" Grace laughed, and was gone.

How does a small business take the next step to become a serious business? It was clear to William when he walked in that it all comes down to the size of the holiday decorations and budget. The wreath on the wall that guests saw first, real evergreen, was taller than a five-year-old. It had tasteful, white fairy lights woven through its branches, but no sign of a power cord anywhere. The Christmas balls were sparse, but, like the wreath, bigger than what normal people could legally purchase. Then there was the horn. It was gold and had a purple velvet bow tied onto it. The horn sat in the middle of the wreath. William, not knowing quite what to do, turned around, returned to the door, and rested his head against the cool doorframe.

A month ago, Sarah Joy had asked William about his memories of early holidays in Cuba, and he'd told Sarah Joy about a brass horn.

"It goes on my tree every year," he explained. "When I was little, my father would be the first down on Christmas Day, and he would blow the little horn, waking my mother and me up so the festivities could begin. His father used to do the same, with that same horn, when he was little. It is unclear how long the horn and tradition had been in my family."

Since his mother had passed away this year, this would be William's first Christmas alone. And there it was, a monument to William's family memories, for everyone to enjoy.

Sarah Joy watched as William noticed the horn. He looked at her to be sure that it really was what he thought it was, not just a decoration. She came over and gave him a second hug.

"Your father was very helpful in decorating for my party, and I'm grateful to him in so many ways," Sarah Joy whispered in his ear.

Damn this woman, William thought, embarrassed that he was tearing up. As he walked around, he bumped into people several times who were stopped mid-stride to look at a picture on the wall, or a knickknack on a table, or a decoration on a tree—they had just stopped and touched and sighed, and usually decided this is where they would sit for awhile.

She had worked hard for these people.

William saw Grace just as she flew by again, and he grabbed her by the waist, practically tackling her. Grace just said, "Carol," and walked away, knowing that he would easily see her, then probably stay and watch awhile.

Carol was moving through the crowd in her Chloe blouse and Prada mules, with a serving tray full of shrimp and small plates—just one of the friends who had offered to help out. Carol is the kind of woman who men look at twice with interest and women look at twice with envy (and/or interest). Her blond hair always looks like it has absolutely never been brushed. William had decided to call it her RITCWHHOTW (riding-in-the-car-with-her-head-out-the-window) look. Her lips glistened for everyone; such a nice little gift! Her pants were very Christmas plaid—the kind that keeps you guessing whether they are high fashion or really nice PJ bottoms. Carol wore a form-fitting white tank underneath an un-ironed pink shirt. Only one button—one very strained button—was at work: at the tightest spot.

William blushed, realizing that the thoughts running through his head were a series of awful, shrimp-related pickup lines.

William desperately tried to refocus, to get himself out of bar mode. He took his eyes off her lips. They landed on her fingernails. Flawlessly done, they were painted with a color that could only be described as "shrimp."

Carol did not sport quite as many ornaments as the Christmas tree in her area, but people noticed the two gold chains that were fortunate to rest on the pale skin of her chest, the two gold bracelets, and the four gold rings. William noticed that no member of the ring collection appeared to be legal and binding, so he expected interest in the shrimp to remain at a high level throughout the party.

Grace walked up and casually patted William's bottom, a move she'd perfected during his first few weeks on the job.

"I thought you were following me," she smiled.

William rolled his eyes for her. He was relieved that she had found a moment when she could stop running.

"I knew that wouldn't happen. There are too many things to see that take time to appreciate," Grace said.

"I just learned that shrimp are really fascinating!" William confessed.

Grace whacked his arm.

"I'll fix your butt," she said as she dragged him to meet a man she introduced as "Frank." Then she vanished into the crowd. William put Frank at about sixty-five. He looked like he had just come from an explosion at the University's gift shop. Frank wore a corduroy University cap, matching shirt with a University logo, and a leather bomber jacket with "CADILLAC OPEN" emblazoned across the back. A plane ticket was sticking prominently out of his shirt pocket. William immediately realized his importance: how nice that he had stopped by, whoever he was—probably on the way to the airport on some important recruiting trip. Grace, however, remembered Frank's visit to last year's party. His uniform was the same, down to the boarding pass.

William found Frank a bit boring, but the boarding pass had writing on it, and reading it became a challenge to

William, so he participated in small talk, all the while staring and squinting at the pass. He became so obsessed that he pulled his phone out of his pocket, lied about being the party photographer, and put Frank next to a tree. He zoomed in on just the list. He then moved on, far enough away to be able to expand the photo on his phone's display. For someone as important as Frank, the list was surely in code:

Vitamin C (500 mg tabs)
Quart milk (2%)
Special K
Apples – 2
Gum
Folgers's coffee

And the last item looked like it was probably "Disposable Lighters."

Frank's clothes said, "Look at me. I am money. I'm an active University alum. I've gone to their football games for thirty-five years. I'm somebody." Frank expected the party to stop due to the excitement of his arrival. It did not, so even the opportunity to nab a shrimp, or talk to William, was less than satisfying to him.

"Hi, William. Don't know if you remember me. I'm Harry. Seen Sarah Joy around? We have a date." William didn't remember Harry, a longtime client there, but was shocked to hear someone mention Sarah Joy and the word *date*! Harry tried to look over the heads of the people to see if he could spot Sarah Joy's hair. William did what he normally does: looked down through the crowd for Sarah Joy's shoes. William won, and sent Harry in her direction. When she spotted him, she took his arm and said, "OK, Harry, let's do some shopping!"

Twenty minutes later, Harry took three bags full of shampoos, creams, earrings, bracelets, hair pins, and aromatherapy candles, all gift-boxed with light purple tissue paper, out to his car. His wife and daughter always appreciate Sarah Joy's good taste at Christmas time, and they don't complain at all that she does so much of Harry's shopping.

Harry leaned against his car for a moment, feeling the cool air and occasional snowflake on his face, trying to reconstruct how exactly he had spent $340 on shampoo and stuff, but like many at the party, he invests regularly in The Conscilience and knows that it's money well spent. He should probably have left, but decided to go back in for just a little more atmosphere.

At this point in the party, the place was full. Get-togethers like this are not necessarily enjoyable. Everyone knows the host, but many people don't know each other. Throughout the year, Sarah Joy often plays a game with people during their appointments. It's called "WELL, I NEVER!" There aren't really any rules—you just talk. Sarah Joy might say, "Well, I've never been to a Disney place, like Disneyland or Disney World." Knowing that her client has teenage children, she then gets to hear about how many times the family has gone to Disney World, and what they did there. So, with a room full of people basking in evergreen, Sarah Joy clapped her hands and made an announcement.

"All right, people, it's 'WELL, I NEVER!' time! Talk to whoever is on your left." The place erupted. William is always fascinated with the things that people come up with. Two people near him said, "Well, I've never used a pen," and "I've never eaten corn." He laughed as people fielded the topics. Larger groups seemed to get into very lively discussions! William just hoped he'd never have to participate, and reminded himself that he needed some WELL, I NEVER!'s in case of an emergency. It's a challenge to decide what about you is a little unusual, and even more interesting to find out if you're right or not! Within ten minutes, almost 70 seventy people were starting to feel like good friends.

Grace grabbed William again, and quietly said, "Check out Sandy over there. She's a good little mafia wife." William felt a twinge of stereotyping embarrassment. Grace hadn't actually pointed Sandy out, but William immediately knew. (If you had any doubts, every time someone sat down with a plate of food, Sandy had to say, "Eh, mangia!")

Sandy's silk, skintight leopard top barely touched her short brown leather skirt, which looked great with her black stockings. Her short brown hair with blonde highlights fit neatly around her thin face and high cheekbones. Her eyebrows were a modern masterpiece—undoubtedly drawn on by a true artiste. Sandy was the only person in the room wearing short sleeves; they were tight and showed off her biceps quite well. Mornings at the gym had definitely been redefining her body, as was her trainer. As sharp as she looked, and although every man in the room couldn't help but watch those legs and that butt cross the room, no one found her drop-dead attractive. Even though most of the people at the party were married or attached, they often came to the party each year alone, and mild holiday flirting maintained a solid sexual tension in the room. At least everyone was smiling for most of their visit. But in this, Sandy neither contributed nor participated. She stayed with her girlfriends and family friends, and was happy to be present without meeting anyone new.

Grace continued to take the job of helping William "meet and observe some party people" seriously— occasionally.

"You know, newly passed state laws require that any gathering of ten or more include one. Today our one is Ray." Grace made a quick head nod in Ray's direction and left a confused William to witness the Ray Experience.

At first William assumed Ray was the focal point of a conversation—probably a real entertaining kind of guy. However, he quickly noticed that, as Ray loudly talked, those around him did not lean in with rapt, undivided attention. Rather, they listed in the opposite direction, floating away as fast as they could without actually jogging. As the crowd around Ray dissipated, his animation did not. Finally he turned toward William. There was a shadow on his face—the shadow of a small boom microphone that grew from his ear, on a vine that twisted down to the phone on his belt. He was talking, and he was loud, but apparently no one here was worth talking to, so he had found someone interesting elsewhere.

Good to have you here, Ray, William thought. Still, he appreciated Ray's look. A handsome, dark-skinned man in his mid-twenties, Ray was dressed to the nines—no casual attire in this man's closet. Or perhaps the double-breasted suit, silk olive shirt, silk purple-print tie, and electronic arsenal *were* his casual outfit. It was good to see that his inability to lead a simple life had taken its toll. His lean body could look great in a severely tailored suit, but the bulges—oh, the bulges: his iPod, phone, and something else small and electronic in a case of its own—

ruined that perfect look. This pleased all within earshot to no end.

To William, Ray's presence was quite the puzzle, because Sarah Joy's clients all have hair, obviously. Ray's head wasn't exactly shaved, but the cut was so short any barber could have done it (and probably did).

William watched the crowd part, as Carol the shark swam toward Ray. "Care to stuff some shrimp in your mouth for the benefit of us all? Oh, sorry, I didn't notice you were standing here talking to yourself so loudly," she didn't say. Instead, she communicated silently and effectively by standing before Ray, tray outstretched, with an expert's look of disgust on her face. Clearly, in some affairs, Ray the businessman was clueless.

Carol's face—along with a dozen flat-lined faces staring at him behind her, like a collection of Christmas Carolers too pissed to move—proved that while Ray was insensitive, he was neither blind nor stupid. A few people actually applauded when Ray left ten minutes later with $280 worth of shampoos, creams, candles, and a fine brush with a mahogany handle. While these people may not all be "nice," they don't hesitate to speak their minds, to do what needs to be done. That became very clear to William.

Ray's headset never came off, because he was the kind of guy who was always ready to leap into action, always on call.

While the crowd appeared unanimous in being unimpressed with Ray, the collective irritation was not only for the benefit of Sarah Joy, whose party he seemed to be dissing, but for a beautiful woman. She never took her coat off, never mingled; she just stood quietly by the front door. No one was ever introduced to her, but rumor was that she was Ray's fiancé. Everyone assumed that her glazed look reflected her severe frustration at Ray's obliviousness to the things and people around him. William hoped that "fiancé" was French for "dump this turkey right after you get your expensive Christmas present." As Ray walked out the door, more than a dozen people stood in the window flashing the "call me" sign. Ray didn't notice. No matter—they weren't for him. Ms. Fiancé did, and the next day she made her first appointment with Sarah Joy. Hopefully Sarah Joy's clients made an impression! But then, Sarah Joy only works with nice people, you know. (For the record, Ray is a neighbor. His butt has never touched a salon chair at The Conscilience.)

"Is this a meeting of the Screw Loose Club," William asked Grace, "or are you only pointing out the characters to me?"

In response, Grace directed him to the scotch-and-ice-cube counter. There stood Edgar: Edgar Burrows, or, as he is commonly known, "Buzzy." He's been Buzzy since he was born, so dubbed by his father, who couldn't remember and never liked the name "Edgar." Why "Buzzy" was easier to remember is unclear. Buzzy is a normal guy: not too fat, not too thin, not too angry, engaging, always a bud when you need one, and he has a smile for all. He has a good marriage and reasonable kids. He has a job working in a factory for General Electric, assembling industrial-size circuit breakers that are used in hospitals.

William introduced himself as Buzzy poured a glass of the hard stuff. He'd loved scotch since he was thirteen, Buzzy claimed, but only nursed that one glass through the party. Buzzy would probably remind you of that friend who lived on your street who went to Catholic school—he learned to wear a tie with a plaid flannel shirt. His dress style is fun and relaxed, one that's all his own. You can tell he's dressed up because he checked his hat at the door.

Buzzy works hard at parties to not only make friends with every male present, but to flirt with every woman in the place—from Carol, whom Buzzy nicknamed "Fish Fingers," to Mrs. Baker, who will be ninety-one on Christmas Eve and whom Buzzy nicknamed "Heartbreaker." One of the severest side effects of being called "Buzzy" by his father is an intense urge to create a nickname for every person he meets. He doesn't create nicknames in general, but personal nicknames that will be just between Buzzy and you. So, like his father before him, while *your* name won't stick to his brain cells, *his* name for you will. It was like watching the Amazing Kreskin as Buzzy left the party. He stood at the doorway and went around the room, not missing a beat. "See you Heartbreaker—you be good; bye-bye, Fish Fingers, catch you next time (*fish – catch, ha, ha*); good to meet you, Giggles; Trash Man! Dude!"

William leaned against a door jam, deciding that he did like scotch, at least based on his very first glass, which he nursed for the rest of the day.

William took a break from studying some of the characters and took a walk around, looking at decorations and ornaments. He found it relaxing to not acknowledge anyone for a while, but just to listen. The partygoers often made him smile, often made him want to stop and jump into a conversation. But instead he just collected random remarks in memory for another time.

"So, your daughter's driving now? How exciting. My condolences."

"Did you actually glue shrimp shells onto your nails, or what?"

"If they're real, I'm twenty-one."

"Yes, I'm from Croatia. Why? Does it sound like a Brooklyn accent, or can't you understand me at all?"

"My wife? Oh, she's home. Sarah Joy cuts my hair, not hers."

"I don't know. Are shrimps fattening?"

"You have to give me the recipe for those cookies, wherever they are."

"My husband? Oh, he's home. Sarah Joy cuts his hair, not mine."

"Yes, I closed on that property just last week. It was quite the intellectual adventure, working with the Grants. At one point, the Mrs. explained to me that they weren't going to spend extra for an underground sprinkler system, especially since all of the flowers that she would be planting would be above ground. It was a hard decision—do I explain it to her, or just tie a cinder block to her ankle and take her out to the river?"

"I only go there for aromatherapy massages or Reiki—you know, that ancient healing-touch therapy. It really taps into my 'ki.'

"Don't touch that."

"God, you white people are so slow."

"I'll only have another beer if there's a sign on this chair that says, 'Use bottom cushion as a flotation device.'"

"I offered to either fail them all, to give them the grades they earned, or to pass them all. To pass them all, they had to listen to me explain a few things to them—things about responsibility, growing up, and personal pride of workmanship. They voted, and I gave them what they chose. Failed them all."

"I need a separate cream to put under my eyes in the day and one for under my eyes at night? Really? And what exactly is a 'refining clarifier'?"

"I know it's goofy, but every night for a month, I lit one of these candles and worked to relax my whole body. Now I light one up and by the time I smell it, I'm *sooo* calm. I swear it works. It's like self-hypnosis with a touch of meditation thrown in."

"I just love your rings. Is it hard to wear so many?"

"I love this place."

A rope of woven holly branches hung above a small purple loveseat on which the Hamiltons sat: sat as a monument to holiday overload; as a monument to people stuck between misplaced responsibility and reality; as a model for what we could all become if we're not careful.

Fifteen years ago, when they moved into the area, everything was exciting. They were excited to move into a diverse neighborhood, to not stand out as the only African-American family on the street. James's job as an architect was exciting; Jane was excited as a homemaker eager to conquer a new house and neighborhood. Now, time is a drag; time drags them through their planners from one appointment to the next. A party is no longer a party; there's no excitement—getting ready or going— it's just one more responsibility, the next thing to do, on an infinite list of things to do. Parties as obligations—it sucks. But they are loyal Sarah Joy groupies, and so they sit. James, tall and graying, always seems to have one hand raised as he pats down the hair lick of his short graying hair while staring off into the room. Christmas lights twinkle and reflect off his glasses as he sits with a full mug of hot cider in his non-patting hand. It is not clear whether or not his body is aware that it is holding something. He sits shoulder-to-shoulder with Jane, but neither speaks. They smile and become animated if approached, but their batteries quickly run down when friendly strangers wander away. Jane's hair is almost as short as James's, save for the long bangs. They almost match, with tasteful grey trousers and dark blue sweaters. Jane's semi-dangly earrings carry blue and grey enameled beads, almost like little Christmas ornaments—if Christmas colors were drab and boring.

Very tasteful. She sits and knits. People look away because it is sad to watch her: tight hair, tight outfit, thin face and body, feverishly knitting. The yarn is black. Usually devoted knitters are not far from their craft; they or members of their family wear the clothes that they knit—especially scarves this time of year. No evidence here. Perhaps she's a beginner. Perhaps a black scarf for James is about to be born, or stillborn. If one gets close enough, at a time when they actually share a few words with each other, the demeanor is as inviting as they look. It is a very sad holiday scene, creating a Grim corner in a good party.

For every yang, there is a yin; for every James and Jane, there are people who go through life like champagne bubbles. Tonight's yang to the Hamiltons' yin is Jan and Deena. William spotted them just as they were moving toward the Hamiltons. He knew them as Sarah Joy's neighbors, as "the Lesbians!" but barely recognized them tonight in their alter egos. William looked at Jan and felt she really could be a model. Her sweater and cotton pants fit perfectly, as if they had no other option. Her smile was professional and enduring. She was relaxed and confident, and could make anyone feel outclassed if she wanted to. But Jan was just happy to be Jan, especially when she was with Deena. Deena was dressed neck to hem in Ann Taylor today. William had never *really* understood why/how hair could be silky, like they always say on commercials, until he watched Jan run her hands through hers.

Jan and Deena could do very well by incorporating and renting themselves out to parties. Of course, they would do parties for free. Jan and Deena are people-people. They arrive at a party. They squeal—not too much or too loudly, just enough to be the epicenter of a crowd. Seemingly driven by dominant shopping and hostess genes when in their professional mode, they make no attempts to fight the urge to make parties *parties*. They play a room as a duet. They descend on prey without prejudice. One minute they'll nab a guy they don't know, attaching themselves to each arm. It's never a "Hi, Handsome" thing, but a "Hi, I'm Jan. I'm Deena. What's your name?" And off they go—fawning over their happy victim until stereo grins claim another victim. If you just heard the tone of the "Hi's," you wouldn't know whether they were clamping onto a man or woman. Everyone is a potential new friend or admirer, and everyone at the party will have their turn being Jan-and-Deena-ized. Sarah Joy walks by and sticks her lips into either Jan or Deena's sweet little ears about once every twenty minutes, thanking them for being them.

William watched as they went after James and Jane, clearly recognized as a major project to undertake. Jan and Deena moved in and made a fuss over the black, formless object that Jane was knitting (stopping short of asking what it was going to be, and if it would be inappropriate for her to actually stop while they were talking to her). Deena told them they looked charming sitting together on a loveseat framed by Christmas. However, even professional people-people can't always break the grey clouds that hang over grimlies. But Jan and Deena have encountered difficult nuts to crack before, and seem to have a Plan B and even a Plan C for every occasion.

After five minutes of their best attempts at conversation with the Hamiltons, Jan and Deena sent a silent signal to each other by a brief look and furled brow. "Well, it was very nice to meet you, Jane," they both agreed. Then, Jan ever so softly pushed Jane to the side just a bit so she could plant a well-glossed kiss on James's cheek. Deena carefully placed one on the opposing side.

Then they silently floated away.

Now filled with helium, James floated to the ceiling. Without a string tied to his shoe, it was hard to get him down. While Jane attempted a look of horror—a very contrived look—and moved to quickly pull him down and erase the lip prints, James raised his hand and spoke his loudest word of the evening: "Don't."

Jan and Deena: mission accomplished. Off they flew, setting their sights on a young teen who was standing alone, looking at some lipstick.

James and Jane had some "words" on the ride home. As soon as they got into the house, Jane told James that it would be foolish to walk around with two lip prints on his face for the rest of his day, so he promptly wiped them off with the collar of his shirt. He had the rest of the day to relive the thrill of stereo kisses, and she had the rest of the day to consider women finding her husband attractive.

That night James and Jane had a surprisingly good time under the covers. Go figure. She put the "dirty" shirt on a hanger in the bedroom where it could be seen, and left it hanging, unwashed, for many months.

Jan and Deena do something interesting, and while not necessary, they do it to keep things simple. They play parties straight; you'd never know, if you hadn't met them elsewhere, what sweet lesbians they are.

Sarah Joy's parties have no beginning. She schedules customers until the announced start time—customers who, she is sure, will stay. She invites a dozen, always a dozen, to a pre-party an hour before. Of course, even pre-parties have a beginning, but they help the caterers and decorators set up and it's never clear who's just helping and who is the hired help. All of the catering staff gets full party rights. So, even if you arrive early, you become a valued contributing participant. These are the best, most well-conceived party beginnings you'll ever see. No one ever feels awkward at a Conscilience party, unless they bring the awkwardness with them.

Usually if you're at the end of a party, you look around at some point and realize the crowd has noticeably thinned. Either you ask the hostess to search for your coat and join the "thanks, gotta go" line, or feel comfortable enough to pour yourself another glass of Argentinean zinfandel. Sarah Joy orchestrates ends. The party always has some final event, after which Sarah Joy can smile, and genuinely look around the room and say, "Thank you *all* for coming. I'm so lucky to have such good friends. Happy holidays to *all* of you." This is her code for "lights out in five minutes." Party ends are not rushed. They take as much time as they need to. Seasoned Conscilience partygoers understand, and they all look for opportunities to be major organizers in a spontaneous party end. This time, in a major surprise, it was Grace. Apparently she had found some time to take a break from party maintenance and visit with some people. William looked around when he heard someone tapping a glass with a knife, in bride-and-groom-kiss style, until people became quiet and attentive. "Ladies and gentlemen: a toast. Please raise your glasses with me. To Sarah Joy and the staff of The Conscilience Thank you for *everything*." The crowd smiled and applauded.

"William, and uh, the rest of the staff, take a bow! You earned it," Grace said as she started waving to everyone. William followed her lead.

Grace continued, "I was just talking to someone that some of you may know. Her name is Jeanne, and she's been telling me a most interesting story that I hope she will share with us all. Even I didn't know the details, and I practically live here!"

"Oh, no," Sarah Joy said, smiling …

"It's OK," said Grace, as she eased Jeanne into the circle that was forming.

"Jeanne," Grace explained, "is a realtor—the realtor who sold this very building to Sarah Joy. Jeanne?"

"Thank you," Jeanne began. "I hadn't prepared a presentation for this evening, but the story is still vivid in my mind and I'd be happy to share it with you all. I won't set business cards out for you all [the group laughed] although I *am* in the book!"

She looked to Sarah Joy, who graciously nodded, allowing her to continue. "This house went on the market with me listed as the contact. It was barely a house, as some of the neighbors remember. As an assistant realtor, I was pissed—I mean, (oops), really angry with the owner. Of course, it was once a fine home, but the owner died and this place, along with the smaller house next door, ended up in the hands of some distant nephew and his wife and family. I never met them, but I heard enough stories. They were from Arkansas, I'd been told, and each had a fifth or sixth-grade education. She was twenty and had had the first of her five kids at age thirteen. Yes, I know I'm being petty, but I've been drinking! How many of you have ties to Arkansas?"

She looked around, to see whom she had offended. Jane Hamilton would have raised her hand, had she been listening, so Jeanne hadn't offended anyone.

"The nephew had hunting dogs, for some reason," she continued. "They couldn't afford to even keep the heat on for long, so they often lived in a trailer out back and used this house for the dogs—two dogs for each kid, I'm told. Somehow, the windows on the first floor got kicked out so the dogs could freely move in and out. It took four years before taxes, bills, and a separation got them to leave the area. Those dogs used this house as a bathroom for four years. How can I tell this story delicately? Urine and feces soaked through the hardwood floors into the basement. Wild animals, large and small—and the weather—did serious damage to the place. If you've ever had a raccoon spend the week visiting, you know what I'm talking about."

Everyone snickered appropriately.

"One day a woman asked to look at the house," she said, feigning a look of surprise. "I expected that we'd not actually come inside, which was just fine with me. But we did. As we walked through, I was humiliated to be showing the place. Plus, the smell was unbearable!"

At this point Sarah Joy stepped up and joined Jeanne. Sarah Joy reminisced: "You know, as we came up the drive, I looked up at the roofline and I knew that, at one time, this was a beautiful home that the owners must have been so proud of. It had such beautiful lines, and an impressive square footage—twice what I wanted. I realized I could not only open a salon here, but I could live here. I just stood in the middle of this very room and pictured all the woodwork refinished, shiny and white. In my mind, I put the windows in, and I could see the room so bright on a sunny day! The walls begged for a dream for them, too. I'd—well, I'd stepped in something, and looked down to see my purple pumps. I knew then what color would be perfect for the walls. The place deserved a second chance. I think it dreamt of one as well, so I decided I could help her. I made an offer, but I never heard back from anyone."

Jeanne spoke up. "She wrote down a number and handed to me. Honestly, I didn't even know what it was."

"It was 25 percent of the asking price," Sarah Joy explained.

"What the hell?" Jeanne teased her. "I was too embarrassed to ask."

"Well," Sarah Joy continued, "I waited awhile, saw that it was remaining on the market, so I asked to visit again, and made the same offer, a little more clearly ..."

"And I accepted," Jeanne added.

"I remember coming back to look at the place for a third time," Sarah Joy continued. "Sometimes I lose track of the time. I just had it in my mind that I needed to look around again. When I called Jeanne she was quick to point out that it was 9:00 PM, but she was gracious and agreed to meet me here. We walked around with two flashlights. I'll never forget one image. We walked in and stood before that window. As Jeanne told you, the windows had pretty clearly been kicked out. A long piece of glass, sharp like an icicle, hung from the window frame and caught the light. From the bottom bloody tip, hung a swatch of gray-looking hair. Probably dog hair. I said out loud, "This is important. This means something," and was immediately embarrassed. Now I knew this line well, Richard Dreyfuss said it in *Close Encounters of the Third Kind*, and I'm sure Jeanne thought I was an alien at this point anyway. I looked up on the wall and saw a mark which I touched. It was a hole. I tried to not think about whether it was actually a bullet hole, or whether it was important as well. I told Jeanne again that we had a deal and that I loved my new house. I must have stared at that ugly, bloody window for quite awhile, oblivious to the cold wind blowing through it. Jeanne told me we should leave, and sounded serious, so I agreed."

"I wanted to leave because, as I was shining my flashlight around the house, I saw the glow of two eyes!" Jeanne exclaimed.

"I never saw them," Sarah Joy said, "but I do believe you, of course."

"It was a wild dog ... or something," Jeanne suggested.

"Bigfoot!" Sarah Joy said.

Jeanne laughed.

"And that worked out well. He's been a good customer." Sarah Joy continued.

"Too bad he couldn't make it today," Jeanne said, as the smiles grew in the crowd.

"Family obligations," Sarah Joy deadpanned.

"So that's the story of how Sarah Joy gave this beautiful house a second life, and how I made an impossible sale," Jeanne smiled.

The group applauded and smiled. Sarah Joy felt warm with so many memories. Neighbors felt the warm feeling of rising property values and smiled. Jeanne curtsied.

Like the end of a church service on a football Sunday, the place efficiently emptied out in seven minutes and forty seconds. William made it a point to be among the last to leave, and got to watch Jeanne and Sarah Joy put out some candles, then sit in two comfy chairs to spend a little more time reliving an interesting time in both of their lives, and to make clear how surprised they were that so much dog poop could have led to such a great friendship. For all the times William had seen Sarah Joy smile *for* someone, it was nice to see her smile for herself.

"Merry Christmas, everyone," William whispered, "and to you too, Dad," as the cold wind blew on his face. He realized that his cheeks actually hurt, he had spent so much time smiling. "And thank you, Sarah Joy."

After this warm personal moment, he also realized that he never had gotten around to his one assignment: to talk to people about his role in The Conscilience and get some massage appointments set up. Ugh!

- 7 -

MEET THE UMSTETTERS

Sarah Joy has attracted some interesting people, and for a hair cuttery, she has attracted an unusual number of couples. Typically, it was always the woman who found The Conscilience first, and her husband, having problems with "barbers" who wouldn't change with the times, came later. Nowadays, of course, men are much more sensitive to their looks and their hair, so often the men come first, and recommend Sarah Joy to their wives. This was the case with the Umstetters. Susan Umstetter does sports commentary, and occasionally covers other stories, for the local CBS affiliate. Everyone knows her because she's on the news every day at 6:00 AM and 5:00 PM. Zac (no "k") is a professional hockey player. They are a busy couple, to say the least, but they have hair, and hair grows, and while they change appointments more than anyone else, it's worth it for Sarah Joy to be part of their lives. Susan is a very busy person, but when you can spend time with her, she has interesting stories. In her time on the air she's met many VIPs. Zac, born in Canada, has played hockey since his father first strapped skates on him, took him out to the pond in the back yard, and handed him a hockey stick. He has played on fourteen teams, from age five to the major leagues. He played for the Philadelphia Flyers for six years before being traded to what Sarah Joy refers to as "the hockey team, you know." A longtime bachelor, Zac got to know Susan when she had opportunities to interview him. Part of the Zac-and-Susan story that is hard to believe is that they could ever manage to date, much less get to know each other. True, it wasn't easy. Weeks would go by when they could not get together. But their authentic interest in each other kept the relationship growing.

Susan and Zac are, from a hair standpoint, interesting people. Susan must have a "fashionable" yet functional haircut. It needs to be able to invisibly morph from one style to another. Zac is unpredictable. There have been times when he and his team members have shaved their heads or sported mohawks, for example.

Most importantly, there is a third member of the household who has hair—Alicia. Alicia is a beautiful, almost sixteen-year-old young lady. Actually, there seem to be two Alicias: one is twenty-one years old, and one is nine. Alicia is an exception to the rule that everyone who comes to the Conscilience is nice. Sarah Joy dreads Alicia's appointments because the girl is seemingly in a permanent bad mood. Having heard Susan's stories, Sarah Joy understands much of Alicia, but it doesn't help. Alicia is hearing impaired. With partial hearing loss in one ear and total hearing loss in the other, life has been difficult for her. The one hearing aid helps, but going through life trying to process all sounds through what sounds like a cheap AM radio is hard for anyone, much less a kid. Without adequate hearing, it is common for children to miss many of the intricacies of daily life and interpersonal relationships. Alicia has had some wonderful teachers, and has learned a lot. But she is not a simple person, and her days are exhausting. While most kids "listen with one ear" in school, she has to constantly *focus* just to get 40 percent of what goes on in class. Even the best-intentioned teachers rarely remember that she depends on lip reading extensively. So they walk around in class, scratch their noses while they talk, turn out the lights and use overheads, talk to the screen—all things that take them out of Alicia's world. She desperately wants to be "normal," and is constantly reminded that she is different. Perhaps adults can "rise to the challenge" every day, but asking a child to do so is asking for more than Alicia can give. Imagine what your life would be like if you never watched cartoons. Perhaps cartoons are not now a part of your daily life, but there are parts of your personality that came from cartoons. You remember characters, you watched them interact, and you listened to their music, their voices. You know who the Simpsons are, or who Mickey and Minnie and Goofy are. If someone refers to Mickey and Minnie, you understand the reference. Alicia does not. Cartoons make no sense to a child who reads lips. Because she misses parts of life, there are pieces of her that are age-appropriate, and parts that are much younger. This is not to suggest that Alicia has not done some spectacular things. She learned to use hearing aids, she signs at the speed of light, and she worked seriously with a very aggressive speech teacher for six years. Unlike most people who have serious hearing problems, Alicia has impeccable speech and pronunciation. One interesting feature, especially after meeting her Canadian dad and local mom, is to hear her sing with a southern drawl. It has to make you smile. This is the influence that a speech teacher born in Louisiana can have. The fact that she sings at all is amazing.

And with this background, prepare yourself, because the schedule book indicates that today is a day when Alicia is scheduled for a visit. It is not always clear how she gets to The Conscilience. Either one of her eternally busy parents drops her off without stopping the car, or household help gets her there. But in she comes—wearing a tight white top, denim overalls, and Adidas, flipping her long dark curly hair. Where the natural tight curls come from is a puzzle. Perhaps the speech teacher.

"Hi, Sarah Joy," Alicia whined as she plopped down in the salon chair.

"Hi, Alicia. How are you today?" Sarah Joy asked, being careful to face her, walking on Alicia eggshells as usual.

"OK."

"How has school been?" Sarah Joy asked.

"I hate school," Alicia stated flatly. "All my teachers suck. I went out for cheerleading. Cheerleading sucks. I hate the kids at this school. They are all snotty, and they stare at me all the time. I hate them. They're just mean, and they don't want to talk to me."

"Well, that's too bad. I know I had times at school when it seemed I just wasn't getting along with anyone. But it always changed." Sarah Joy tried to be encouraging.

"So?" Alicia responded. "Can we talk about *my hair*?"

"I would love to talk about your hair," Sarah Joy smiled. "What would you like to do today?"

"Well," she sighed, "Mom wants me to keep my '*long, beautiful hair.*' She can keep it in a baggie if she wants it. *I'm* sick of it. It takes forever to wash, forever to dry. I just hate it. Can you cut it off?"

"Well, sure, we can talk about some shorter styles," Sarah Joy said nervously.

"Why won't *anyone* do *anything* I want?" Alicia moaned. "This is *my* hair. Shit. Cut the damn hair off."

"I'm sorry if you're upset, Alicia," Sarah Joy said, gritting her teeth. "I'd like to keep you *and* your parents happy.

Do you want to look at some books on hairstyles? I'll bet we can find a cool one."

"Why do all adults have to be a pain in the ass?" Alicia snarled. "I've seen the books before. The books suck. Look, can you cut, like, a few inches or something off my hair? And these bangs are in my eyes. I want them shorter, but not too short. I don't want to look like a geek."

"I can do that," Sarah Joy said. "Why don't I cut off a few inches and we can see how it looks? If you want a little more, we can keep going."

"I hope so. We are *paying* you for this, so you have to do what I want," Alicia reminded her. Sarah Joy certainly appreciated the lesson in running a business and serving the public. "I'm not leaving if I don't like it."

Sarah Joy chose not to respond. It killed her to act this way, but she wasn't about to be bullied—well, not *completely* bullied—by a child.

Now, one of the first things you have to do before you cut long hair is to wet it down and comb it out. With thick hair like Alicia's, combing it out can take some real muscle. Unfortunately, Sarah Joy made a mistake—a mistake that anyone else would have dealt with, but in this case, a mistake that was an excuse for Alicia to go ballistic. As Sarah Joy pulled the brush through her hair, the bristles hit Alicia's left ear. This ear is not just any old ear. It holds a hearing aid. *The* hearing aid.

Alicia yelped, "*God damn*. That's my hearing aid! You just suck. Why can't you watch what you're doing? You're not very good, you know."

At that point, she reached into her ear, pulled out her hearing aid and threw it across the room. Sarah Joy has heard Susan talk about the price of digital hearing aids, so her heart stopped when pieces flew from the collision with the wall.

From here the visit went downhill. She never did calm Alicia down. Alicia made a call, spoke three words into the phone ("Come get me"), and sat outside. Someone must have heard her. Sarah Joy didn't know how Alicia would even have known if someone was coming to pick her up or not, with her hearing aid pieces stuffed in her pants pocket (that she was sitting on). But someone did come, because moments later, she was gone.

Sarah Joy does not always have a good time at her job. She was sympathetic for Alicia, but would have been willing to strangle the girl.

The next morning, Sarah Joy asked William to call Susan at work. He called seven times before they caught her in the office, and her secretary was willing to put the call through to her.

"Hello, Susan," Sarah Joy said. "You probably know that Alicia and I didn't have a very good visit yesterday."

"Oh, really?" Susan was authentically surprised. "She wouldn't talk when she came home, and I noticed that she didn't have anything done to her hair, but she didn't say anything. I'm sorry. She can be very difficult at times. Things are just not going well for her at school right now."

"Yes, she told me that," Sarah Joy said. "What really concerned me is her hearing aid. It broke into pieces. Can you fix it?"

"The little bullshitter," Susan laughed. "Oh, I think it's OK. I didn't have a problem talking to her this morning. It's fine."

"I don't think so, Susan," Sarah Joy warned. "She got mad at me, pulled it out of her ear, and just threw it against the wall."

"My poor Sarah Joy," Susan sympathized. "We paid extra, a lot extra, for what the audiologist called a robust hearing aid. Battlefield ready! We also pay a lot for insurance for when she leaves it somewhere. Even when she throws one of her little tantrums, the throw-the-hearing-aid act is very controlled. She throws it just right, not too hard. She knows how to do it very well. The little door pops off and the battery pops out. Three pieces every time. It fits right back together—all done for the theatrical impact. Next time offer to throw it for her. You'll see! She won't let you!"

"Well, I guess I have a lot to learn," Sarah Joy admitted.

"Well, hon, if what you learn is to stop making appointments for Alicia, we'll understand." And with that Susan became a dial tone.

- 8 -

I WITNESSED LIPFEST
as told by guest reporter, Melissa

I am one of the few women to have ever witnessed a testosterone-filled event that takes place annually at The Conscilience. It is known to the inner circle of participants as "Lipfest." I appreciate the opportunity to provide this story. It was a difficult decision on the part of Sarah Joy to allow this information to be known. The name has been changed to protect the fun-loving.

I guess I hadn't thought much about it when Sarah Joy agreed to cut my hair one February night at 8:00 PM. I didn't know that she normally closed at 8:00; I was just really pleased because I would have had to miss work if I had come earlier. It had been a busy couple of weeks, and I was looking shaggy.

Appointments late in the day at The Conscilience are nice because it's just you and Sarah Joy, and some of the staff cleaning up. I was looking forward to quiet time with her. We had just finished my wash and mini-head massage when I heard the front door open. A guy came in—nice guy in his forties. He walked through, hugged Sarah Joy, and went back to the little kitchen counter she'd just put in the hallway that was next to the stairs. I could hear him rifling around in a drawer; then I heard a cork pop. He reappeared with a glass of wine in one hand and some red and white M&M's in the other. He was introduced as Brian, one of the judges. I had never noticed, but every year, starting around the third week of January, Sarah Joy starts her collection. She cuts out hundreds of paper hearts, and collects lip prints from as many of her women customers as she can. Each one has a number on it, and she keeps a list of who kissed which number on a clipboard that is usually hidden somewhere. By now this year's collection had become substantial; hearts were everywhere, taped to large mirrors in three of the rooms. It was her "Best Lips of Valentine's Day Contest."

Slowly, they appeared. Five guys, all very different, all very funny, all named Brian, wandering through my private time with Sarah Joy.

"I get them together every year," Sarah Joy explained, "give them something to drink and some snacks, and just let them do their thing. Don't tell them, but it's my Valentine's Day gift for them too! They pick the best lips, and I give out some prizes, little goodie bags, to the winners."

"It must be hard to agree on the best out of two hundred pairs of lips, don't you think?" I asked. (What I was actually thinking was, *They don't have a lip print from me! Can I do one now?* I realized I was already getting a bit of a gift as well, so I decided to just smile.)

"Actually, I usually tell them to pick the top four, but they always disagree with me and pick five or six or ten," Sarah Joy told me. "They are good guys. They are men who love women, so they would be happy if I told each and every woman that *they* won, that *they* were picked. One year they wrote 'WOW!' And 'MMMMM!' on lots of them, just hoping the women would get some positive feedback. 'Every woman wants to know that someone thinks she's special,' they tell me. I have a hard time disagreeing, and they know that.

"And they're a riot," Sarah Joy continued. "Two years ago, their first choice ended up being one of my older clients. She was about eighty-five."

"Hmm? Oh, I'm sorry." I felt embarrassed, but I was just imagining the whole process, and not listening. "What? She was what?"

"She was eighty-five," Sarah Joy repeated. "At first they were unsure how to respond to the fact that the sexy lips they picked out belonged to an older woman, but they got over it in a hurry, and were pretty pleased to know that an eighty-five-year-old honey was going to be told she was their top choice."

Brian walked through and told us to make sure we didn't come into whatever room they were in—not the first Brian, and no, not Brian the bear with the Gabby Hayes beard; it was the short, older Brian with the earring. He complimented Sarah Joy on her selection of M&M's and wine, and glanced at my lips as he walked by.

"There are snacks too!" Sarah Joy felt compelled to explain to me, loud enough for him to hear. "It's not just M&M's."

"No, no, M&M's go really well with a merlot. I've read that somewhere," he shot back as he ran through.

"Oh, get out of here!" Sarah Joy giggled.

Sarah Joy then continued her explanation to me. "So anyway, then last year they were doing all of this stuff about sexy lips and ..."

"They ... what?" I blinked.

"What was I saying?" Sarah Joy asked. "Oh, they were doing all of this stuff about sexy lips and it turned out that one of the lip prints they picked belonged to Brian's daughter. She was twelve. We had to restart his heart! He swore he couldn't look at either lipstick or his daughter's lips for the next six months. Clearly, I hadn't thought to monitor the entries closely enough. I just assumed that everyone who had left me a lip print, whether I was actually in the room with them or not, was an adult. We eventually determined that Brian's daughter came with him one day, and during his haircut, she must have been playing with the lipstick, and one thing led to another. I guess I'd left my clipboard out and she wrote her name on it."

"Uh-huh," I replied.

"I'm sorry, I'm losing track of my own conversation," Sarah Joy finally admitted. "I'm just listening to these goofy guys out of one ear."

"I was just going to say the same thing," I happily confessed. "They seem to be having a lot of fun together."

We looked at each other and simultaneously suggested, "Why don't we just listen?"

And so we did. From bits and pieces of the conversation, I'm guessing that one was a professor, one was a neighbor who worked for Blue Cross, and one organized events related to photographic exhibits. We couldn't hear everything, but we laughed a lot just listening to them laugh. Every comment was followed by lots of giggling from both the guys and us two eavesdropping girls. Of course I couldn't tell the Brians apart from their voices, but I didn't care. Sarah Joy and I were having too much fun.

This is what we heard, or at least a reasonable recreation:

"OK, Brian, you've done this the longest, what's your plan for this year?"

"Well, why don't we just look at them all and we can each pick our top ten? Just put your mark on one if you want to vote for it; then we'll work on those."

"My mark? I have a mark?"

"Just pick something—a check, a star, something. Be creative, man!"

"Ten marks each? We could end up with fifty lips?"

"No, it doesn't work that way. You'll see."

"We need to make this as scientific as possible."

"Think Sarah Joy has a protractor?"

"I don't even think she has enough rulers for us to do this right."

"I can't do this if we're not using metric."

"So should we have some criteria or something?"

"No, that's part of the process. Different aspects are important to each one of us. Of course, after we assign some scores, we'll have to do a statistical analysis and calculate standard deviations."

"I think Sarah Joy has Excel on her computer. We can graph the results."

"Let me just make a case for this one. Don't you think that's an incredible color?"

"Hooker red?"

"Right. You mean the color of a professional … uh … ?"

"Right. I meant professional. Is that red or what? Definitely hard to ignore. You have to be interested in a woman who buys and wears *that* color of lipstick."

"I thought we were going to have the live lips here this year."

"Maybe they're all in the back room."

"No, I checked."

"Rats."

"This one is nice. You can tell she was smiling when she made the lip print. Very cool."

"Oh, yeah. Smiling is good. Sarah Joy has to start giving out instructions with these things to the kissers. Some women just press their lips against the paper, some clearly kiss the paper and give you that kewpie doll/Barbie doll shape—and then there are these."

"The blow-job ones?"

"Yeah, they folded the paper over and stuck it in their mouth like they were soaking up extra lipstick with a napkin. When you unfold it, you get this round ..."

"This one looks big enough ... I mean for me, you know."

"Yeah, right!"

"OK, I think we're done with round one. Let's collect all the ones that we picked and put them together."

"Well, perhaps we should move them all up to our lip level so we can judge them better."

"I was thinking we should put them lower."

"I think you're working on a theme here?"

"OK, round two. From these that we've chosen, each of us should select three, so put a mark on your top three. They don't have to be ones from your top ten. Just take a fresh look at this set we have now."

"Oh God, please, no geriatrics and no little girls!"

"More wine?"

"Are there M&M's left?"

"No, just brie."

"No M&M's? Where is she?"

"I'm just kidding. Of course there's more M&M's."

"See this one? She has some lipstick on her moustache."

"It's probably the FedEx guy's lips. I swear Sarah Joy is in love with the FedEx guy."

"What's his name?"

"Brian."

"Ha ha ha ha ha . God, she's got a problem!"

"You know, I *like* the feel of lipstick. Maybe *my* lips are up here somewhere."

"If you got it, flaunt it."

"Is this a great shape or what?"

"It is, but why is there a spot missing?"

"Scar tissue?"

"Looks like."

"I think this woman was probably in a fight at Arnold's Bar and cut off part of her lip on a broken beer bottle."

"Oh, yeah, I think I was there when that happened."

"Me too. Yep, the beer girl has luscious, full lips."

"So do we get to take a few of these home? You know, if you're having a bad day, you can pull one of your favorite set of lips out of your glove compartment and, you know, spend a quiet moment with them."

"Hey, if a heart falls off and into your pocket, whatta you gonna do?"

"Exactly."

"Exactly. But if you like it that much, don't you want her to be a winner?"

"We'll have to come back for our booty after Valentine's Day."

"Good luck negotiating that with Sarah Joy."

"I can handle her! No worries."

(Intense male laughter.)

"More M&M's?"

"Thank God she didn't try and pull the old white-wine-with-just-M&M's-trick."

"Oh, look at these. Are they real? How can someone have lips this big?"

"Color, guys, you're not focusing on color selection enough."

"I knew we shoulda had a training session first."

"I'm into the shapes."

"How does this work? I thought everyone had one of those little dimply things in the middle of your top lip. How do you get a lip print like this?"

"I think you're holding it upside down."

"Oh. Yeah, that works. Damn, this is a good merlot."

"Doesn't this look like a sphincter muscle print?"

"Well, thank you. Now I've lost my taste for the M&M's."

"Sphincter? Like in Egypt?" (Snort.)

"It looks like that because she actually kissed the heart. She didn't just touch the paper to her lips, she *kissed* it."

"Still looks like a butt print to me."

"You're a butt print."

"Gentlemen, let's move the ones that didn't get any votes in round two off to the side. Are we ready to come up with the top four?"

"No way. Sarah Joy just doesn't want to give out gifts. We have to at least get to pick five women as the best lips this year. And the other two hundred—she has to swear that she will tell each of them that they were runners-up."

"Definitely. Why don't we each just pick our personal favorite? Then we'll have five. But five still sounds like a small number. Let's tell her that we could only agree on the top ten."

"High five."

"High ten!"

"OK, time for some serious decisions here."

"This is hard work!"

"I'm sure if we give her ten lips, each one will get a nice little goody bag of makeup crap, and some message she'll make up from us. She can afford it."

"Do we all agree on these? Does everyone have one excellent choice in here?"

"My number-one is the lips with the little smile."

"Hooker, I mean, professional lipstick. Can't get the color out of my mind. That's mine."

"Bar girl. She's my top pick."

"These here are just so amazing to me. I pick them just in the hope that someday I can find out who actually has lips this big."

"And the big-O open-for-business one here is my favorite."

"Gentlemen, we have done our job."

"I hope she throws some M&M's into those goodie bags!"

"If she complains at all about having so many, we can suggest that she could just take back the brie to pay for it all!"

"There was brie?"

"Yeah. That's what they call that cheese whiz stuff in there."

"Wasn't Brie the redhead in *Desperate Housewives*?"

"Do we have any duct tape around here?"

"Now that we're getting the hang of it, we should be thinking much bigger."

"We could do this at eight to ten places in the area. You know, become THE JUDGES."

"That's still small. We need a website: Lips.com. Women, or people, just anyone, could submit their lips, and our peeps would vote on the web for the best lips of the month."

"Oh, yes, this is good. We could get someone to write a smartphone app to capture lip prints, and then they could be downloaded and sent to us. We need to go to Daytona Beach and get on some cable channel like SPIKE TV. 'The Lips.com guys are out on the beach again!' Sarah Joy would need to spring for the Lipmobile. We could wear our Lips.com T-shirts (with lip prints over each nipple), collect lip prints from babes on the beach—we'd be hot."

"We really *could* do Lips.com. It could be interesting— lots of lips to look through from people, voting for new best lips every week, constant turnover, tie it into some of Sarah Joy's products, Lips.com T-shirts and hats, maybe even leather jackets. Do you think we could get Mick Jagger to do an ad for us?"

"Isn't he dead?"

"We'll need a theme song. What is a song that was written in the past fifty years that has 'lips' in the title?"

"Hot Lips?"

"That's Hot Legs."

"Lips Get in Your Eyes?"

"That's 'smoke.'"

"We can write a song. We only need eight or twelve bars. So, are we in? I don't have anything special scheduled for this spring. Lips.com at spring break?"

"Well, I have things scheduled for spring, but that doesn't matter. I'd change it for this."

And on they went, silly guys kidding about Lips.com, wondering if anyone else *really* felt like there was the gem of a good idea here, no one willing to consider it seriously enough, but all knowing that they'd probably dream about lips tonight. It was just interesting to hear five handpicked guys together. They joked like they were brothers, like old friends, even though Sarah Joy told me that some of them only see each other once a year for this, and one was judging for the first time. It's interesting that not only is Sarah Joy so good at identifying compatible people, but also that she has such a substantial pool with which to work.

I felt very fortunate to have been able to listen into the process that night.

And that concludes my report.

Kisses!

M

- 9 -

SPEAKING OF STARS

Sarah Joy had essentially cut half of William's hair when Grace interrupted his fascinating story of "My Grandmother's Green Hair."

"I'm sorry, Sarah Joy, but Susan Umstetter is on the phone. She needs to talk to you."

"Needs? I hope she doesn't need to reschedule—again." Sarah Joy looked at Grace. Grace didn't know.

Grace persisted. "She wants to talk to *you now*! And you know Susan; she doesn't waste time with words. Whatever it is, she's only going to say it once."

"Go ahead," William said. "How much can my hair grow in a few hours?"

Sarah Joy took the phone from Grace's hand.

"Susan? Is there a problem?" She made it sound like she was taking this interruption very seriously, so it had better be. "Who? Oh, yes, I see. You mean *now*? *Now*? Well, I have a full schedule for the day, but ... OK, yes. She's where? Well, yes, certainly. A favor for you. You know I'll do what I can. OK. OK, bye."

"A favor, huh?" William said, as she returned and started brushing the hair off his shoulders. "I have a funny feeling it's going to be a quick haircut today. Just give me some sharp scissors and I can finish it in my rearview mirror."

Sarah Joy explained: "Susan is covering the visit of Calluna Blackheart to town. She's going to be doing a few fundraising events, and is spending a day visiting some schools in the area. Calluna's hair apparently needs some attention, and needs it now! She was visiting a second-grade class at Grant Elementary School, and a little girl got her gum caught in Calluna's hair! Do you know who she is?"

"Well, the name sounds familiar, but I can't say for sure," William admitted.

"Calluna was Miss America a few years ago—the second Miss America with an impairment. Remember her? She can't hear, and danced ballet for her talent," Sarah Joy reminded him. "Everyone talked about how she was so incredible, dancing without hearing any of the music."

"Oh, yes, how could I forget?" William exclaimed. "So she's coming *here*? A Miss America at The Conscilience? Can you take a picture of me with her?"

"I think she wants a little privacy," Sarah Joy said as she treated him to a little scowl. "Out you go! We'll finish you tomorrow sometime."

"Fine," William pouted. "I'm nobody. I can walk around here looking stupid for a day."

"Good plan," Sarah Joy replied, trying to focus on how to handle a celebrity visit. She handed William the scissors she was holding. He hoped she was just a little flustered, and wasn't assuming that he was serious about finishing his own haircut in the car. She patted his bottom, nudging him out of her salon room.

What is it with these women and bottom patting? William thought.

William's back started to ache from trying to do anything in his car, but he almost had his bangs done when he watched a limo pull up. It was Calluna! William was surprised that he actually recognized her. He jumped out of his '84 Honda Civic and sprinted to the front door.

Calluna got out of the limo with two suits—both interpreters. They frequently embed themselves in crowds around Calluna so that whenever someone speaks, Calluna knows. She knows where to look, and talks to people in a way that feels natural—until you realize that someone is standing behind you signing everything you say. If she is facing you, she will probably read your lips; otherwise, her handlers sign to her what you are saying.

Calluna has worked extremely hard to interface naturally with the hearing world. She hears a little bit, and she speaks unusually well for a person at that level. But she still speaks like a hearing-impaired person, so she prefers to speak through someone else.

William held the door open as her two people walked past him and Calluna Entered! (She didn't "enter"—she "Entered"!). The boys quietly placed themselves in the room—they were efficient and exact in every movement, and looked a bit like Secret Service. William expected them to speak into their lapels.

Calluna, who wore a crisp, dark blue cotton dress with a fur collar, beamed and shook Sarah Joy's hand. When William saw the outfit, his mind, for some reason, tried to picture a chipmunk's funeral.

Calluna signed, and the guy facing Sarah Joy spoke for her, "It's so nice to meet you, Sarah Joy. I can't tell you how nice it is of you to do this for me. I've had such a frantic schedule lately. You're a lifesaver."

"Well, Calluna, come into my styling room. What would you like me to do?" Sarah Joy asked.

Calluna grabbed the wad of gum stuck in the back of her hair, and Sarah Joy winced. "Don't worry, Calluna, I'll take care of it. And if it's OK, just let me trim your bangs a little. The rest of your hair will be fine for weeks, but I just want to take a little tiny bit off."

Calluna nodded and smiled. The interpreters failed to sign that last little sentence because they were helping her put her gown on (her salon gown).

Sarah Joy stared at the two-thousand-pound elephant in the room, not knowing what to do next. Ever since she had arrived, Calluna had been carrying a polished mahogany box in front of her, using both hands. She sat with it in her lap.

Sarah Joy tried her best quizzical look, to see if a well-played facial expression might work. It did.

"Oh, yes, of course, the box," Calluna said. "It's my crown! I thought you'd like to see it. Everywhere I go, I take it. When I was Miss America, it traveled over twenty thousand miles a month. Lots of people ask me about it. Would you like to hold it?"

And so, as requested, Sarah Joy called in Grace and William to spend some time meeting the crown and its owner, and making an appropriate fuss.

"Would you like to try it on?" Calluna asked William. Funny girl. He didn't want anyone looking at the top of his head in any way at the moment, so he let Grace do the honors instead. Everyone smiled.

Overall, the visit was a good one. Calluna talked about growing up in Seattle, about some of her hearing-impaired heroes, and what it was like to travel around Europe representing the US. She had doubtless had these conversations thousands of times before, but her job is to glow until she dies, and she does. It is rare that you meet someone who actually warms a room with a smile. Calluna doesn't, but if she asks, you'd be well-advised to tell her that she certainly does.

It wasn't until very late in the visit that the subject of Alicia came up.

"I have a hearing-impaired young lady client, and I know she is really having a hard time. She misses a lot in school but doesn't want to admit it; in fact, she misses a lot of life and doesn't want to be hearing-impaired, so she is just angry all the time," Sarah Joy said, then immediately worried that she had jumped in with too many details too soon. Calluna didn't act like she knew that Alicia might be Susan's daughter, so Sarah Joy felt a little better.

"Oh, that is so sad," Calluna signed to an interpreter, who stated it in real time. "Does she wear hearing aids?"

"Yes, she has one," Sarah Joy sighed.

"Well, that is good, because it means that she is taking care of herself," Calluna proclaimed optimistically, with her man's voice. "She has not stopped trying."

"Last time her hearing aid was here, it shattered when it hit the wall," Sarah Joy told her.

"Why?" Calluna asked, as if she had never been a hearing-impaired teenage girl.

"I made the mistake of touching her hearing aid when I was cutting her hair. That just set her off," Sarah Joy explained, wondering why she had even brought it up.

"Can you tell her I was here?" Calluna asked.

"Of course," Sarah Joy said. "She'll be sorry that she missed you."

Calluna's hand reached out, and immediately it held an unusually large black-and-white glossy photo. In her other hand, a marker appeared. These interpreters were well-prepared! Sarah Joy wondered if they were taught by Diane Grim's handlers!

"What is this young lady's name?" Calluna asked. Her sentences were formal and a bit awkwardly constructed, and it was clear that her interpreter/handlers worked hard to make all conversations come off as natural.

"It is 'Alicia,'" Sarah Joy said, as she watched the interpreter fingerspell the name.

On the picture she wrote: *To Alicia. Please know that you will always be a part of me and I will always be a part of you. I love you. Calluna, Miss America.*

"Oh, Calluna, I'm sure she will love it," Sarah Joy over-bubbled.

"Well, she'll love it, or she'll tear it up. Life is hard for all teenagers. It is not easier when you are hearing-impaired." More proclamations from the girl with the crown. "Can you see my hearing aid in the picture?"

Sarah Joy had to look closely. "What? Where? Oh, yes, I can."

"It is the most important part of the picture," Calluna explained. "It is just a little triangle there, just a very small thing. But people who know see it. It means a lot to them. I had to make sure people would see it, because they need to know that this is what I use to help deal with the world around me. That, and two very well-paid interpreters. There just wasn't room for them in the pose." She smiled at them and they silently grinned, then signed "laughing" back to her. When she looked away, they rolled their eyes at each other over the "very well-paid" comment.

Grace and William never left the room through the whole gum extraction and bang trim. They just sort of—well, they just stood there, all bug-eyed, like they were in the presence of the Queen of England. As Calluna was getting up, showing a special smile of appreciation for her trimmed hair, Grace spoke up.

Sarah Joy had assumed that Calluna was in a hurry, but Grace was caught up in the moment, and suddenly wanted to talk! "Calluna," Grace said, "I've seen Alicia in action here, and whenever she visits, we all try hard to keep her in one piece, but she seems to be so fragile and we always seem to break her. Is there a story that you could tell us that might help her? Maybe one that a teenager might appreciate? You know how girls are—the last thing they want to do is to listen to an adult blab on about working hard and following your dream."

Trying to diffuse anything in Grace's words that might upset Calluna, Sarah Joy said, "Grace, that's not true. Alicia told me once that she read a book by Calluna for school. It was her selection. She wanted to see what an adult had to say."

"Oh, Grace, I know that what you say is true," Calluna said. "My parents killed me a few times when I was a teen. I guess I could tell you a story, but for me it is embarrassing." She turned to William, as did the interpreters. To him she said, "Could you leave us please so I can talk to the girls?"

William cracked a smile, tried to tell Calluna that it was great to meet her, and accepted being sent off, again! A big hug, quite the surprise, made it worth it.

"Bet you can't sign a hug, eh?" he said to one of the interpreters and grinned. It may have been the first time William had said the word "signed." He suddenly felt like he was in such an alien place. (The next day Sarah Joy saw, tucked in the back room, a paperback book: *Introduction to Sign Language*. William had finally decided to get serious about learning it. More than once from then on, Sarah Joy found William in the basement practicing the alphabet. If he couldn't sign many words, he could fingerspell them one by one. William is good people.)

With William gone, Calluna started to talk in a low voice. Actually the interpreters came in close and spoke in low voices. Sarah Joy didn't think there was a low-volume signing system, but somehow Calluna told her interpreters to keep it hush-hush. It was very sweet, and she had a story to tell—a little story that she doesn't tell when invited to give speeches.

And so they began. "I was almost nineteen when I got my first hearing aids. For most of my life, people told me that I had so little hearing that hearing aids would do no good. Then a doctor decided that they might be worth a try. They might help me to pick up a little more sound. It was good; there were lots of things to almost hear that I had not almost heard before. I confused everyone when I started dancing! It was all because, with my hearing aids, I could pick up a little bass—just enough to understand what rhythm was.

"I remember the day very well," she continued. "I was in my apartment. It was morning. I heard a noise with my new hearing aids. I didn't know what it was. I checked the phone, checked the door, and checked the oven. I even checked the refrigerator. I didn't know if a refrigerator had a sound or not, but I had to check. What was this sound? So many things to learn. That same day, that evening, I went to a party. I was with a group of friends. I knew there was a guy behind me, but I couldn't see his lips, so I was trying to talk with the people in front of me. So many sounds, so many people talking at once. My brain cannot process very many overlapping sounds. It is just all noise for me. But through it, I heard this noise again. So I hollered. I was so excited. There was that noise again. The one from my apartment! 'Everyone help me. I just heard a noise. What was it? I really have to know. Help me people! What was it?' It was—it was ... I don't know what to call it. It was a spider burp."

The interpreters laughed. Sarah Joy and Grace were clueless. "A what?" Grace asked, making a face.

Calluna sighed, then signed, "Oh, I knew this was going to be the hard part. I don't even use the word. What do you call it? A fart?"

Sarah Joy wanted to put her hand over Grace's mouth, but it was too late. She broke into laughter. "Oh, Calluna, you heard a fart for the first time? Ha ha ha!"

"Well, no, I heard a fart for the second time," she said, since she's a very literal girl. "The first one was in my apartment and I was alone, so I guess it was mine!"

Then Calluna tried to make a fart sound by putting her lips against her arm and blowing. "This poor boy behind me was so embarrassed, I guess. All I remember is asking and asking what I'd heard, then seeing him head for the door, and then having a friend of mine explain it all to me. When you don't hear sounds you don't appreciate that some sounds you can talk about and some you can't."

"Oh, Calluna, you're a gem," Sarah Joy exclaimed. It just popped out. Just like a fart would.

"I told you girls this so you can share it with Alicia for me," Calluna made clear. "Thank you for making me feel comfortable enough to tell it to you. I love you both."

Calluna loves everyone; that is clear. But it's OK. She is so genuine that you really want her to love you. There are not many people who can spend five minutes with you and then tell you that they love you, but Calluna loves the world, and the world has already made it clear that it loves her back. (Love loves love, you know.) It was a feel-good moment; however, there may *possibly* have been just a few seconds, when Calluna first saw herself in the mirror, that seemed to change her smile. Grace noticed it and decided she was just imagining it, but it looked like a smiling scowl. It quickly passed, like gas, quietly, from Calluna's sweet bottom. Miss America's farts don't stink, of course. Now you know.

Big hugs, and out the door she went. Sitting on the counter there appeared three crisp one-dollar bills. Each one was boldly signed—"I Love You! Calluna"—in black marker ink. One might feel a bit uncomfortable at getting three dollars for a haircut; however, the autographed bills were clearly designed to be of value some day. Each was lovingly placed in a hard plastic sleeve. Sarah Joy loved hers. William loved his. Grace thought about carrying hers with her all the time, in a big wooden box.

THE OTHER HAIR: MISS FLORRIE

William was surprised to find that The Conscilience had a website, surprised that he was on it, and surprised that the "new employee" blurb had his picture, which he didn't remember being taken. He smiled at a line indicating that Sarah Joy was available on a consulting. His first thought was that Sarah Joy was a bit of a dreamer, and always tried to be all that she could be, but a hair consultant? *Does Chevrolet hire hair consultants to design headrests?* He wondered what other talents she might have. But he already knew. He remembered that the other day he had overheard her say on the phone, "It is odd to work on a head when it is not attached to a body, but you get used to it." It was upsetting to him, but he hoped he had no idea what the conversation was about.

There was a time when wigs were big—big as in popular, big as in Parton. Women *had* wigs. Tucked away in bedrooms across the country was an army of plastic heads: decapitated, bodiless heads—homes to the owners' party wigs, or their I-don't-want-to-do-my-hair-tonight wigs, and, of course, their sex wigs. Wigs were in the Sears catalog when there *was* a Sears catalog. Now they are largely found in Salvation Army stores, sought out the last week of October. However, a culture exists, an underground culture, down past the roots, where wigs remain serious business. Sarah Joy is an active wig expert—certified and trained. The clients come from an emotionally bimodal group. They are the women with little or no hair. The chemotherapy patients sometimes openly elaborate on their good fortune to be alive and bald. But the personal strength required to proudly pass through life on this planet as, or with, a bald woman is exhausting. No amount of personal courage makes it easier for a fifteen-year-old daughter to walk through a shopping mall full of peers with a hairless mother. Then there are those who have rapidly thinning hair, women who no longer recognize the face in the mirror. They have tried casual approaches—a new obsession with hats or bandanas—but no casual approach goes unnoticed. Most of these women have passed through emotions including puzzlement, confusion, anger, fear, embarrassment, and depression before they find out, if they ever do, that there is help. This is a group of loners. They don't nod knowingly as they pass each other when they shop. They are not a club. They are an anti-club. All of them who know Sarah Joy have been through a process with her, have bared their heads to her, inside and out. They have cried with her.

Florence Tuckwood, now known as Miss Florrie by all at The Conscilience, got one birthday card on her eighty-first birthday, from Sarah Joy and the salon. She thought it odd, getting a card from a strange place that she'd never heard of. A friend of Miss Florrie's had asked Sarah Joy to send this as a personal favor, knowing that cards are sent to all clients. When Miss Florrie called two years ago, she was not seeking help. Actually, she was desperately seeking help, but could not bring herself to say the words over the phone, so she scheduled a cut as a new client. Surely a hair person would know if there was something she could use to stop or reverse the defoliation.

The hair on her pillow was now rivaling the amount of hair on her head. Talking to her doctor, a longtime servant and friend of the family, was not an option. Was he blind? He knew she was losing her hair. If he didn't mention it, there was surely no solution. *Take a lifetime of silence and call me when you're sick.*

This is not to suggest that Miss Florrie hadn't tried everything she could find. Her books and catalogs suggested vitamin E, which she nightly applied to her cranium. Her book on apple cider vinegar was very encouraging, so she rubbed and rubbed until the tears flowed—vinegar tears and salt tears. All of the experimentation only led to discoloration of what little hair remained. Hair loss seemed to mirror weight loss in her shrinking circle of friends. It was hard to tell, but her frail four-feet-eight-inch frame was a poor carrier for the dresses she draped over herself.

She'd try a suggestion in any obscure reference she could find. Once when a plumber was fixing her bathtub, he found behind the wall an intact newspaper from the year the house was built. In it, on page A8, a small box separating stories simply said "Cantaloupe stops hair loss." For two weeks, Miss Florrie ate cantaloupe every morning. For the next two weeks, she rubbed cantaloupe on her head every afternoon. (The instructions were not very specific.) And every evening, she would recite her mantra. Miss Florrie had a saying—oh, heavens, not for anyone to ever hear. Her friends—at least those still breathing—would surely cease being her friends if they ever heard her say it. This was a personal therapy mantra. She would sit in her living room chair, adjust the doilies on the arms, take her Bible off the table and put it in the drawer, stare at the wall and say, "Getting old sucks." Sometimes it was a chant. Some nights it was a weak but angry cry. Miss Florrie didn't know exactly what the phrase was a reference to, or what it meant, but she had heard so many people say it ("sucks," that is), with such conviction. It appeared to be very freeing, and for her, it was. But what exactly was the sucking part about? She could only think of a vacuum. "Getting old is like a vacuum cleaner" didn't make sense to her, but sometimes you have to go with what sells.

Her mantra didn't make hair grow, but it was, possibly, a way of going to the complaint window. Maybe God was listening—or maybe, she guessed, the language was too foul and made God turn a deaf ear. She will do what She will do (God, that is), as will Miss Florrie.

Miss Florrie was punctual—pulling into The Conscilience parking lot precisely at 1:30. William had cringed (three times!), watching her drive, watching her park, and watching her shuffle up to the front porch. Her cane pushed the front door open by 1:35, and entered before she did. Her wicker hat with the sunflower on it was old but effective. The brim was large enough that the staff couldn't see her and she couldn't see them. Sarah Joy turned on her afternoon charm—this was a new customer, and Sarah Joy has a special warm place in her heart for Helens. Sarah Joy noticed that the hat didn't naturally come off when Miss Florrie came in. Sensing there was something more going on here, Sarah Joy decided to move slowly. With age and loneliness comes finickiness. She was, however, not willing to completely ignore this wicker wall. When Miss Florrie was close enough to Sarah Joy to hear her, she could not make eye contact because of the brim. So Sarah Joy bent down so she could look Miss Florrie in the eye.

"How are you? I'm Sarah Joy. It is good to meet you. I think I know a friend of yours—Helen Winslow?"

"Oh yes, Helen," Miss Florrie said. "She is a dear."

(Silence.)

Older women are experienced at sitting for long periods of time, saying nothing. Miss Florrie's silence pushed aside Sarah Joy's pauses—ate them for lunch. So here they all were—bubbly Sarah Joy, and a short little stick in a purple dress, and a big hat, clutching her purse and cane, in silence.

"Would you like to see where I cut hair?" Sarah Joy asked finally.

Oh my, that did sound stupid. She's not here to get her tires rotated, Sarah Joy thought.

Sarah Joy took a step back. The hat took a step forward. And so, hat, bag, and stick were lured into the styling room, where Miss Florrie hopped, actually hopped, up into Sarah Joy's chair.

Sarah Joy was working hard to handle the pauses. Miss Florrie was unable to do anything. She felt frozen. She couldn't move, feeling too embarrassed to leave. What did Sarah Joy know—had she offended Miss Florrie? Is Miss Florrie waiting for Sarah Joy to make a move? Neither saw what to do next. Both jumped when William came in the front door, tripped over the floor trim, passed through the styling room, and headed for the storeroom. A box of 143 wood-handled brushes skittered across the floor. Mahogany—yes, that was the color. William's face was approaching a pretty good shade of mahogany. For a stocky guy, he scrambled with amazing speed to capture these critters before they made it into other rooms—corralling them back into their box. William looked up, saw a new face, and forgot about his entrance.

"Hi, I'm William. I work for Sarah Joy. Here, let me take your cane for you and hang up your hat."

Whoosh—off they went—the hat over to a brass hook on the wall, and the cane disappeared somewhere out of eyesight with William.

Before he left, he looked at her and said, "Welcome to the family."

Off he scurried. He had looked her right in the eye like there was nothing unusual.

(You know that feeling: you are introduced to someone in a wheelchair with no legs. *Please, God, let me just say hello. Make it a hello like I regard them as a person. Don't let my eyes divert to their legs. Don't let them see me sneak a peek. Please don't let me make them feel self-conscious, just this once. Amen.* If you think this went through William's head, you'd be wrong. He didn't notice her hair at all.)

William smiled, and moved on so quickly he did not see Miss Florrie begin to cry—cry very hard.

One may envision a number of approaches for Sarah Joy at this point. Get to know Miss Florrie a bit, let kindness get the situation under control. But not this time. Even Sarah Joy was surprised when the personality that emerged from her, to deal with poor frail Miss Florrie, was such a take-charge attitude.

"I have no interest in cutting your hair right now," Sarah Joy said. "Why don't we go back out to the front desk and we'll reschedule your appointment?"

"Oh (sob), I'm so sorry, I ..." Miss Florrie said. Words! It was a start.

"Miss Florrie," Sarah Joy said, looking her in the eye, "we've just met, but I would guess that your hair is very upsetting to you. I am going to help you. We are going to fit you with a wig. You will look great and feel even better. I promise you, we can do this. I want you to come in as my last appointment some evening soon. We will be the only ones here. I promise you'll be one of my satisfied customers."

Miss Florrie was flooded with emotions. *A wig, she thought. How could a simple solution have been so far away?* One reason is that wigs always look fake, always stupid. Miss Florrie pictured herself beneath a pile of horsehair sliding off her sweaty scalp, curls dragging on the ground.

"Oh my, no," Miss Florrie protested. "I don't want a silly wig. I'd look awful. People in wigs look so silly."

"No, Miss Florrie, you won't be getting a silly wig!" Sarah Joy said. "People with *bad* wigs *do* look awful. People who do it right look natural. I'm good at this. Can you trust me? If you don't like what I do, there is no charge, and you can walk away."

Now William, who wasn't about to leave the scene, was sitting like a mouse in the back room, shaking his head. He's unpacked enough FedEx boxes of wigs to know that this is an expensive proposition —and you don't return a custom wig. You do your job and order one correctly. He knew Sarah Joy was faced with, potentially, a substantial loss. But for both of them, little Miss Florrie was, for that instant, the most important thing in the world. William sat in a quiet panic—he didn't like what was happening for some reason. It was all too fragile. Miss Florrie could bolt or just never return. He had to take matters into his own hands. Even if he got into trouble or made a bad decision, he had to do something. He started to shake, something that he hoped no one ever saw. His hand shot to his side, plucking his cell phone from its holster. He hit FN 9 (silent mode) and punched in the phone number of The Conscilience.

The phone at the front desk rang, and William ran through the styling room to get it, nearly knocking both women over. "Hello, The Conscilience, this is William speaking. Yes ... uh, huh ... I'll have her call you. OK? Bye, Helen.

"Sarah Joy, that was Helen, she needs to stop by and get a little repair on her wig. Can you call her when you're done with my girlfriend here?"

Miss Florrie picked Thursday night, tomorrow night (!), at 8:30.

Sarah Joy thought about this one a lot. After Miss Florrie left, she lit into William.

"You can't do things like that!" Sarah Joy seriously scolded him.

"I was trying to help," William explained.

"But not with very personal information about other people," she yelled. Of course, Sarah Joy was in control, but she felt she had to raise her voice to make him understand how important this was. "People expect me to run a professional business here. You've compromised that for me."

William was very confused. It turns out that he had picked a name out of the air. He didn't *know* there was really a Helen (other than William and Grace's code word), and he didn't *know* that the real Helen knew Miss Florrie, and that Helen wore a wig. Coincidences tend to stack up at The Conscilience.

The next day, at promptly 8:35 PM, Miss Florrie was back, once again cane-first through the door. She was clearly trying to be strong and confident, and was clearly wrestling with it all. She had promised herself she would be an adult about taking care of her little problem. However, the anxiety of the unknown had made her clam up again. She did, however, at least come prepared.

Miss Florrie had brought in pictures of herself, which was a great idea! She silently handed these over to Sarah Joy, who made an appropriate fuss over them. Miss Florrie was very excited to learn every detail from Sarah Joy on how wigs are made, how hair is selected, how wigs are held on. They drew up plans and experimented.

Seven weeks later, a chatty Miss Florrie walked out to her car with a smile, bangs, and her head upright—and no hat. Miss Florrie never mentioned to Helen that she knew, but spent many hours marveling at how good Helen looked.

During her many visits since, Sarah Joy and William have learned quite a lot about Miss Florrie. She, of course, always visited with her straw hat (now carrying it) and her cane, and of course always *had* to have her hat before she left, and William almost always *had* to bring her the cane, or she'd forget it. They noticed that she walked just fine without it.

William was desperate to have Miss Florrie be his friend. He would do or say anything to try to get her to smile. One day, William walked in on Sarah Joy and Miss Florrie. He was hobbling along with Miss Florrie's cane—just a silly thing, trying to make her smile.

"That's not a toy, Junior," Miss Florrie scolded him.

William sighed.

"You break that, and I'll be eating Ramen Noodles," she continued.

Sarah Joy gave her a puzzled look, so she explained. They learned that Miss Florrie teaches a self-defense course. William thought she was kidding. A nephew from California, always concerned that he just wasn't here for her if she needed him, had sent her a most unusual Christmas gift a few years ago. It took her an hour to open the taped-up box that contained her cane and a book. The book was first published in 1912, written by Andrew Chase Cunningham, and was called *The Cane as a Weapon*. It was an entire self-defense system making use of a "walking stick." She explained that Cunningham was both an engineer for the navy and active in the sport of fencing. Apparently someone expanded the book by making it a combination self-defense system and basis for an exercise program. Miss Florrie took her nephew's concerns seriously. She was an independent woman and had no intention of getting mugged. But, realistically, she knew that she didn't have the strength she used to have, so she learned the program and followed the cane-based workouts. One day, while trying to show a few moves to a friend in a nursing home, she noticed that she was surrounded by an audience, many of whom had canes. She offered to teach them exercises (mostly) and a little self-defense (just for fun). Three months later, she was actually getting paid (well-paid!) for her lessons, offered as formal community college classes. She taught in a room in a local casino, which loved offering classes to seniors as much as they enjoyed being bused there!

Both Sarah Joy and William smiled just thinking about their little Miss Florrie swinging her cane around, and the bulging muscles that she must have hidden under that dress. William made the mistake of smiling at the wrong time.

"What's your problem?" Miss Florrie asked him.

"So, you're teaching classes, are you?" William stated, not sure if he believed it or if she was pulling her leg.

Looking up from the floor, William checked the back of his head for blood.

"And that's just Chapter One!" Miss Florrie said, looking down the barrel of her weapon at him as he lay on the hard wood.

As she left that particular day, William had just taken an Advil, and opened the door for Miss Florrie. Instead of his usual "be careful out there," he just said, "Badass." Without raising her head, she stopped, patted his bottom, and said, "You're damn right I am! Sucks, doesn't it?" And out she went. She didn't even care if that was an appropriate use of the word. It felt so right.

William chuckled for the rest of the day. Miss Florrie walked to her car, wondering if anyone made a leather jacket in her size.

Shortly after Miss Florrie's wig wear became official, she stopped by and left a present for Sarah Joy—a beautiful box wrapped in the Sunday funnies. Only after Miss Florrie left did Sarah Joy open it. This very old Miss Florrie hat, one that belonged to her mother, still hangs on the wall of The Conscilience.

- 11 -

TREATS AND TRICKS
HAPPY HALLOWEEN

Sarah Joy had gotten a good night's sleep and was actually ahead of schedule when she came down the stairs twenty minutes before her first appointment on this Saturday morning. She was so proud of herself. She stopped halfway down the steps to see that William was sitting behind the front counter talking on the phone, their box of client cards open. They made eye contact— an awkward moment—and William said a hasty and quiet good morning/good-bye as he flipped the box closed and hung up the phone.

Trying to get information in a playful way, Sarah Joy said, "And what's this about, William? Is it a girl? Something you want to tell me?" She stopped short of asking if it was a client, although it was fairly clear that it was.

William explained all he could to her. "Nothing," he said flatly, and walked away. Sarah Joy walked into her styling room, pretending she was getting her scissors and combs ready, then came back out and unlocked the front door. She slipped the salon's cordless phone into her smock and went into the bathroom, where the display told her that the last call was made to ... Gary or Claudia! As interesting as it would be to find out that William was seeing Claudia, if there were any affairs going on, it wasn't going to be with one of her staff! Sarah Joy decided that since this was a big Saturday night, with her staff as well as Gary and Claudia attending, she'd watch and see who was winking at whom, for starters.

She convinced herself that she was surely worrying over nothing. It could have been William ordering wine with Gary. But if that were the case, he would have said so. *It's surely harmless.* Sarah Joy just wished she knew what was going on.

Sarah Joy had a perfectly fine day. She found a way to tell each client a story about a little black hat with a short black veil on it, which had to be at least eighty years old. She knew who it had belonged to, and why it was interesting, and spent the day working on story embellishments.

Late in the day, Sarah Joy was on her computer, rushing to order more dye that she needed for a client next week. She knew that Grace was without a client, so Sarah Joy yelled to her, "Hon, can you tell me who's next on the schedule? I haven't had a moment to look!"

"Maybe we should just let it be a surprise," Grace said after looking at the day's list.

"Why?" Sarah Joy laughed. "Who? Who?"

"Umstetter," Grace replied. She said the name slowly, like a death sentence.

"Zac is coming in?" she smiled, "Why are you making such a big deal ... oh!"

There was an extended pause.

"Alicia," Sarah Joy said. "It's Alicia. Well, I'm sorry, but I'm just not prepared for her today."

Grace continued, "She's coming in to get some highlights. I talked to her mom about it and I can do them so you don't have to deal with her this time, Sarah Joy. I haven't had to deal with the wrath of the Princess in awhile."

And just at that moment, said Princess arrived. Her mane was bigger than ever, more impressive than ever. She is a beautiful girl, with beautiful hair. The boys at school must go gaga over her.

Grace's appointment, Joyce, a middle-aged woman with a very active imagination, arrived early and was excited to learn that Sarah Joy would be cutting her hair today instead of Grace, but was quick to ask if the price was going to go up. She was delighted that it would not. So, as Sarah Joy attempted to cut Joyce's hair, she also was listening with at least one ear to the conversation between Grace and Alicia. Most of the talk was about the former Miss America's visit. At first Alicia seemed disinterested, but that quickly wore off. Since Joyce's cut was a mindless one, and since Alicia's highlights take a little longer than a cut, Grace didn't tell the whole story, assuming that Sarah Joy would want to finish it when Joyce left.

Sarah Joy took a deep breath, slapped on an impressive smile, and walked into Grace's lair. "Hey, Alicia! I know that Grace was telling you about our little visit from Miss America. She told us a story that she wanted us to share, but only with *you*."

"With me? Why?" Alicia was authentically intrigued. She acted like a regular person for a second.

"Well, I don't know," Sarah Joy said. "It was hard for her to tell it, but it was important to her too—important that we share this story with you!"

Sarah Joy began, "Calluna didn't get her first hearing aids until she was almost 19 years old." And so the story was told, straight through to the fart punchline. Alicia looked inquisitive and listened intently, but never interrupted.

Alicia stared at the space between Sarah Joy and Grace in silence—not a Sarah Joy Pause, but an Alicia-silence. Then a funny thing happened. Tears started. A noise started to ball up and roll out of this kid.

Oh shit, now what? Sarah Joy panicked. *If she gets violent, she's never coming back through my door. I don't care who her parents are.* But the noise evolved—evolved into a good sound. A laugh. A good old hearty laugh. A squeal on top of a laugh.

Oh, my God.

She got it.

"She told you *that*? Just for *me*?" Alicia squealed. The more tears ran down her cheeks, the more tears ran down Sarah Joy's cheeks, and she didn't even know why.

"Just for you, kiddo," Sarah Joy smiled.

It appeared that there was a kid inside—a regular teenager! She had been touched by someone who had gone through the same things. Maybe she wasn't alone. It was a powerful message. Calluna knew what she was doing.

Feeling like she was on a roll, an incredible roll, Sarah Joy said, "Oh yes, and she left a picture for you too."

Alicia got quiet, not believing what she thought she heard. "What?"

Grace just couldn't stay quiet any more. "A picture! She left a picture for you!"

Sarah Joy disappeared. She grabbed the photo from a drawer, grabbed a very nice frame from her styling room wall, and quickly put the photo in this oversized frame. She ran back in and handed it to Alicia. She read the writing on it aloud for her.

"To Alicia. Please know that you will always be a part of me and I will always be a part of you. I love you. Calluna. Miss America."

No one ever checked to see if there was a mark left on the ceiling, but all reports suggest that Alicia jumped from the chair. Hair flew. She moved toward Sarah Joy so fast that Sarah Joy barely had time to brace for the collision. It was a hug, a big hug, delivered just right. There was enough good stuff left to make one for Grace, too. Well, that changed everything. Maybe Alicia was growing up a little bit. Whatever the case, the girls were beside themselves. If you have a dog that bites you every day, and one day it licks you and curls up with you, you appreciate that special time. Grace and Sarah Joy appreciated what they hoped could be the new Alicia.

"Before you go, I want you to try some things," Sarah Joy said as they walked out into the front room. Sarah Joy was so happy, she wanted to shower Alicia with gifts, and started to grab everything she thought a teenage girl would love. But, for some reason, it just didn't feel right. She wanted to celebrate this moment, but not pay for it. She let Alicia pick out a few lipsticks, and gave her a nice shampoo. Off Alicia went, very happy with her surprise goody bag. For once, Sarah Joy looked forward to Alicia's next visit. For once, Sarah Joy felt that all was right in the world, and that all of her clients were, in fact, nice people.

As Alicia was walking away, she looked back to the side window and saw William watching her. He reached out his right hand, and pulled it toward his chest. Then he flipped his hand over his shoulder. Then he pointed to an imaginary watch on his wrist. "Come back soon," he signed. He had been practicing that. She smiled, not knowing that, inside, Sarah Joy just hollered.

"William, get her back!" Sarah Joy yelled.

William ran out to Alicia's car (her present for her 16th birthday) and knocked on her window, scaring the crap out of her. Afraid that the tide would change, he quickly said, "Sarah Joy wanted to see you for something else before you leave," and ran back inside.

No damage was done by William spooking her, apparently. She came back inside with a smile, and found Sarah Joy.

"Alicia, do you have plans for the rest of the day? It is Halloween, you know. I'm having a séance tonight. Would you like to stay?"

After saying the word a few times for her, and (surprisingly) having William fingerspell it for her, Alicia had no idea what it was, so Sarah Joy explained that it was a thing that people do to try and communicate with dead people.

"You do this on purpose? Why?" Alicia asked.

Good question. Sarah Joy just shrugged—she didn't really know how to explain it. "It's a Saturday night, when sometimes I have clients come in to party, and it's Halloween!"

For the second time today, Alicia went happy! "Yes, yes!" she said. "I hate Halloween. My friends are all at the age where some want to go roam around in the dark, others don't. I'd really love an excuse to avoid the whole thing."

"This could get scary," William cautioned her.

"Yeah, right!" Alicia replied. "Whatever!"

The staff got Alicia comfy with some magazines to read, and Sarah Joy checked the schedule book to see who her last client of the day was. A new client—Kathie Odessa. She had made the appointment three weeks ago. Odessa ... didn't ring a bell. Well, she soon learned that there was no Kathie Odessa.

It was a fake name. Undercover. Right on time, Millie walked in, and from then on, became yet another Conscilience groupie.

"Millie, I'm so happy you are here," Sarah Joy sang as she gave her a big hug.

"Well, my heads are a big hit now because of you. Plus, you owe me a story," Millie said. "You had told me that you *do* work with dead people, but you never explained what that meant. We just started working. Cut my hair (!) so I can finally hear what you were talking about."

There are times when an hour cut is done over small talk. Sometimes, Sarah Joy is the psychologist, more than happy and prepared to listen. Also, on request, she is more than happy to provide a monologue. Millie just opened door number three, requesting a story never told by Sarah Joy before.

"When I was in beauty school, there was a girl named Renée," Sarah Joy began. "Renée came from a town almost two hours away—she was a real out-of-towner to the rest of us. One evening some of us went out for pizza and Renée started to get to know us. She told us about her Uncle Ed, who died while serving in the Air Force. He loved old service planes, and signed up when he learned of a unique opportunity to do some WWII plane renovations for the National Air Force Museum in Ohio. He was bolting empty bombs on the wing of a B-52 when the bracket cracked, broke, and he was crushed. His body was sent home and young Renée was dragged by her mother through every detail of preparing his crushed chest for the funeral. Renee made her plea. 'I want each of you to do this for me—think about what you as a beautician will do when someone asks you to do work on a dead body. I want you to give it real thought, anticipate it happening, and tell me when we graduate what you decide. I'm going to ask each one of you.' And she did. Most of the girls honestly said no—just couldn't do it. I said 'yes,; and made it a solemn pledge. I was grateful that she made me think about this, and four times I've been called. That's why you had the luxury of having your consultant dive right in instead of getting the vapors over the vapors of the lab."

"But, how do *you* ever get to work on a deceased client? Just tell me about one," Millie asked.

"In a weird parallel to Renée's Uncle Ed, I have a client named Eleanor," Sarah Joy explained. "Eleanor's daughter Rachel was killed and severely mangled in a motorcycle accident while away at college. Her body was sent home and Eleanor called me, asking for my help in getting Rachel to look like she did before the accident. Imagine, at the brink of physical and emotional exhaustion—you call someone for help. What would it have been like if I had said no?"

"And ... ?"

"And—it was horrible. As you know, it is bad enough when the coroner has parts to pick up. What I hadn't known about is how a punctured body responds to a plane ride," Sarah Joy said.

"Yes, if the skin is not intact, decompression can suck body parts out of even a small cut," Millie replied.

"I worked with the undertaker, but Rachel was never going to look like Rachel again. I spent eighteen hours with that guy, trying everything, making measurements, calling some pretty creative people I knew, but in the end I had nothing. It was a closed-casket funeral—but I felt good that I could be there for Eleanor. I tried, and she knew that I cared.

"I only saw Eleanor once more," Sarah Joy continued. "I think I was just too much of a reminder for her of Rachel. It's too bad. I really enjoyed her, but I understood."

"Well, as I've said before, I'm very impressed, Sarah Joy," Millie smiled.

"We all have a bit of a secret life, eh?" Sarah Joy smiled.

"No," Millie said. "Not me. No secrets here."

"I told you a story, so you owe me," Sarah Joy said.

"Deal. And thanks for the cut. How did you know what I wanted? Don't you *talk* to clients about what they want before you start working?" Millie grinned.

"Oh, yes, but we were talking and I guess I just knew," Sarah Joy said, somewhat embarrassed.

"You *knew*?" Millie continued to harass her.

Millie's hair was still a little black helmet—just six weeks shorter.

Sarah Joy gave Millie some stupid line about how every client's first cut is free—it's a tradition at The Conscilience, and Millie accepted the favor. As Sarah Joy scheduled Millie's next appointment, she handed her a green cat's-eye marble.

"What's this?" Millie asked.

"Oh, sometimes when something special happens here involving a client, they get a marble. Occasionally marbles can be traded in for other things."

"Quite the little operation you have here," Millie chuckled.

A pause was in place—a Millie Pause. She looked out the window and got a little smirk on her face. She knelt down on one knee, pulled her pant leg up to mid calf, and snapped a small flat silver handgun off a leg holster. Alicia looked up, hearing a sound that she didn't recognize, saw the gun, and came right over.

Sarah Joy saw the gun, and saw Alicia moving toward it, and couldn't believe Millie was doing this! She moved fast but Alicia got to her first.

"Can I hold that?" Alicia asked. Sarah Joy intervened, to slow all this down. She made introductions as Millie, snapped and clicked her cute little weapon back into place.

"I'm sorry, baby, it's not registered," Millie explained.

"Who do you work for?" Alicia asked.

"The state police," Millie replied.

"And you have an illegal gun? You're a bad girl," Alicia said, smiling. She high-fived Millie.

Sarah Joy found out why Millie had gone through this exercise when she handed Sarah Joy a bullet. A marble for a bullet. Quite a trade.

"Here, six of these and you can fill a gun barrel," Millie smiled.

Sarah Joy gets warm and fuzzy quickly, and knows an expression of emotion when she sees one. She gave Millie a warm hug.

"We're going to be good friends, aren't we?" she said to Millie.

"No doubt," Millie responded.

Sarah Joy asked Millie to stay as well for her Halloween event, and while they were waiting for it to start, Sarah Joy, William, Millie, and a very comfortable Alicia—comfortable because she was being treated like an adult—stood around and talked. Millie explained to Alicia how she and Sarah Joy had met, and told her some things about her job. Then the conversation got serious.

"You know, Alicia, when we try to reconstruct someone, I *never* thought about whether the person wore hearing aids, so I've never made a head with one. This could be an important detail!"

Alicia immediately understood, and explained to Millie about behind-the-ear and small digital hearing aids, even cochlear implants. She showed Millie what kinds of marks and indentations her hearing aids made on her head and ears, and showed her what a typical battery looked like. Millie agreed that she should be familiar with such details.

"No one may have *ever* had this conversation before," Millie said excitedly. She was impressed, and handed Alicia her card. "Can I call you if I need you, if I ever have a question?"

At that very moment, Alicia beamed and made some important career decisions.

While Sarah Joy never really appreciated the importance of the work that she and Millie shared, Millie did get some national recognition during a critical project, and she was very excited to make certain that Sarah Joy was recognized as well. One of the high points of Millie's career came ten weeks after she first worked with Sarah Joy. Some of Sarah Joy's ideas for adding hair to clay were developed further by Millie. Millie was still proud to not be an artist, but a mechanic. She developed somewhat of a theme that Sarah Joy talked about, to look at pictures and people to understand shapes and curves that naturally exist in all faces. All of this led to Millie's ideas being pursued by the curator of the Department of Anthropology at the Smithsonian's National Museum of Natural History. In July, Millie made a presentation in DC at the Biennial Meeting of the International Association for Craniofacial Identification. The title of her talk was, "Facial Reproduction and Photographic Superposition in Forensic Anthropology." It listed three authors: one from the Smithsonian, one from the state police, and one from The Conscilience. Even Alicia was impressed. Sarah Joy was some kind of secret scientist! So cool!

Having a séance was actually Grace's idea, so Sarah Joy invited the staff, which worked out great, because it almost didn't happen. She had Gary and Claudia scheduled in. Two of her Brians had been invited, but their wives wanted them at home to help hand out candy. Now she had Alicia and Millie. Seven is the perfect size for a group. A deliveryman brought some shrimp, cold cuts, rolls, crackers, dip, and a variety of drinks just at 5 PM. Sarah Joy squeezed the four into her salon room while she worked to prepare the séance room—the basement. It was the only room with no windows, so it was perfectly black when needed. She hadn't planned on having many props, but she spotted the *Pagan Book of Halloween* by Gerina Dunwich at a yard sale. This guide to "magick,"from healing and harmony to incantations and spells, also included a great pumpkin muffin recipe. She put it on the floor with a rubber tarantula on top. She then ran up to her bedroom to dress up—sparkles in her hair, sorcerer's hat, and a black gown. Last night she had put iron-on ghosts onto a few salon smocks. A CD of creepy sounds was put on the sound system. Screams, cries, chains, moans—all just set in the background. Seven chairs were placed in a circle with a star (a triangle overlapping a square)—all drawn in fluorescent chalk on the floor—seven chairs, seven points. She moved Alicia, William, Grace, Millie, and the food to the basement, and for the next hour and a half, she cut Gary and Claudia's hair. Her basement victims had strict orders that they could not speak, so there were constant giggles from downstairs as they whispered to each other, trying to make sure Sarah Joy wouldn't hear. Sarah Joy got them started on crackers, stuffed mushrooms, peeled grapes, shrimp, cheese, and lots of wine. She poured a Cherry

Coke in a wine glass for Alicia. Millie let Alicia have a drink of her wine. It only took one sip, and Alicia decided that alcohol might not be for her.

There was a second text—an old book she had found in the shed out back, a big, leather-bound, badly stained book. She copied pages out of the incantation book and glued them into the big old book. Fortunately, one thing that The Conscilience is *not* is haunted. No ghosts roam the basement or the halls. Nothing there goes bump in the night.

Sarah Joy led Gary and Claudia down the steps, seated them, and lit the black candles that were on the floor at each star point, in front of each chair. Now the room was full, everyone in a circle, candles flickering. The last blow dryer had been turned off as well as the rest of the lights in the basement. Since everyone wore a Halloween smock, one could only see floating heads and glowing iron-on ghosts. Sarah Joy floated—well, tried to—around the room to begin, a fluorescent glow stick in one hand and her book "clutched to her bosom." (She loved that phrase.)

The crowd hushed.

Sarah Joy stopped floating and joined the others seated in the circle. She opened her book of spells to a page marked with a black ribbon, looked around the room, and used her best spooky voice.

"We are here tonight to contact those from the other side," she spooked.

The group giggled. Then the candle in front of Sarah Joy flickered out. Everyone got seriously quiet. William relit it.

"Chant with me," Sarah Joy said to them all as they joined hands without being told. She put the book in her lap. "Spirits from beyond, we beseech thee. Come to our gathering. Speak to us."

"Spirits from beyond, we beseech thee. Speak to us," the others chanted.

Close enough, a spirit in the corner thought to herself.

"Spirits from beyond, those at our gathering wish to speak to a loved one, someone on your side now. They each have a request for you. Spirits, help us!"

Sarah Joy then turned to William, who sat next to her. Sarah Joy had not exactly explained how this was going to work, so he sat for a while, thinking, then realized she was waiting for him.

"Uh, oh wise spirits, I am William. I wish I could talk to my grandmother, Megan O'Toole, who passed away ten years ago."

Surprised that they had to speak, Gary was next in the circle.

"Oh wise spirits, I am Gary. I would like to speak to my brother, who died of cancer when I was young. Please grant my wish!"

Claudia went next. "Oh wise spirits, Claudia is my name. I would like to speak to Mrs. Miller, my longtime neighbor whom I loved very much. She died last year when an eighteen-wheeler hit her. She was so sweet, I'm sure her soul must shine."

Next in the circle was Alicia, who had been sitting, almost frozen, with her head looking down the whole time. She slowly looked up. Her face was pale and so shiny.

(You should probably know that this group doesn't sit in silence ever! They had been quietly scheming a few surprises for Sarah Joy earlier, and this was one of them. They had lightly sprayed Alicia's face with hairspray. The way it reflected light from the candles was eerie. Creepy. Damn scary. She looked so much like a dead person that Sarah Joy's heart jumped. Millie's did too, even though it was her idea.) Alicia kicked William's shoe and winked.

Sarah Joy yelped when she saw Alicia, then her goose bumps got goose bumps as Alicia's lips started to move and a man's voice came out. "My grandmamma. I need to talk to my grandmamma," William said as Alicia moved her lips. Then her head drooped again. This was seriously creepy stuff in the flickering candlelight.

Before Millie could take her turn, Gary spoke up. "I can."

Sarah Joy turned to him, puzzled. "You can *what*, Gary?"

"What's gotten into you?" Claudia asked him.

Sarah Joy, following what she'd read about séances, said to Gary, "Who are you?"

"My name is Michael," Gary replied. "I can help you."

No one said a word. They all shared a strange panic and a common interest to desperately figure out what was going on. Gary's wife, however, did not appear to be having fun.

William was quick to say, "Let's do it."

"Michael," Sarah Joy asked, "who are you?"

"I ... I'm not sure," Gary said. A slight accent could be detected. "But I can hear you and I seem to be able to touch lots of people. If you think of them or if they know you're with me, I think I can help you talk to someone."

"OK ... Michael, we'd like to talk to someone we know."

Alicia exhaled and took a deep breath. She then farted. Sarah Joy looked at her. After a brief Alicia Pause, she said, "Spider?"

Claudia wished she hadn't had that fourth glass of cabernet.

Sarah Joy screamed. She pulled her hands away from those on either side. In the dim light, something that looked like a bat flew through the room, but stopped on her lap. She screamed again and pushed it off her, into the circle. It was a hat—a hat that fell from the shelf above Sarah Joy's head, into her lap. *Fell* is a poor choice of words, since Sarah Joy's back was hardly against the wall. She was four feet away. This was too much for Sarah Joy to deal with, as was Gary when he began to speak.

"Sarah Joy, she's close. Someone wants to be with you for a moment," Gary said.

Everyone clearly heard the sound of the basement door opening, and footsteps starting to come down the stairs. Creak, creak, and creak. Then they stopped. If you strained your eyes in the candlelight, you could see two legs.

"Who's there?" Sarah Joy demanded, her voice quivering.

"Michael," William said. "Who wants to speak to us?"

"She wants to be with you, Sarah Joy," Michael/Gary said.

A fragrance filled the room—one Sarah Joy explained was associated with the owner of the hat.

"My name is Elizabeth Modell, Sarah Joy. You knew me as Grandma M."

Sarah Joy took a breath and knew. Elizabeth Modell died several years ago, and Sarah Joy's mom got Sarah Joy one of her hats for the shop. She was such a great woman, whom Sarah Joy had known when she was growing up. Elizabeth was, among other things, one of the cooks at her elementary school, and then later at her high school. Everyone loved Elizabeth. All the kids called her Grandma M. She was a family friend and a woman for whom hundreds of kids had a warm spot in their hearts and bellies.

Of course, no one else in the room knew who Elizabeth Modell was. How could they? They did know that the aroma in the room was a complex combination of food smells with a little perfume on top.

"Grandma M, thank you for cooking for us every day. We loved you so much," said Sarah Joy.

The smell changed to peanut butter and perfume. For Sarah Joy it was Elizabeth. No doubt.

Gary smiled. Then he appeared to have been pushed, almost thrown off his chair. He would have hit the candle if Sarah Joy and Claudia didn't grab him. Then he relaxed back in the chair.

"So, anyone want more burgundy?" Gary said.

It was over. Sarah Joy wearily walked over to the light switch on the wall, right under the steps. Her heart flipped as she looked up the now-lit steps. No legs, no feet. Whoever was there was gone. The next half hour was spent explaining to Gary what just happened. Alicia declared she had to pee now! She ran up the steps. When she returned her face looked perfectly normal. Sarah Joy explained to everyone how it had to be real, since the hat that jumped off the wall shelf belonged to Grandma M. As the Saturday night came to a close, it was Sarah Joy's turn to pee, and up the steps she flew, to her own bathroom. Alicia gave everyone a bug-eyed "what-the-fuck-just-happened" look, surprisingly hugged Millie, and headed for her car. Grace secretly thanked neighbor Pam profusely for helping out—for sneaking into the house, taking a few steps into the basement once the séance was under way, then slowly backing out and quietly leaving. She gave Pam a small bottle of perfume for her performance. Pam was thrilled, and happy to be part of anything spooky.

Ending. William walked out to the car with Gary and Claudia. First, they complemented William on his nifty little "hat shooter," made with two pieces of cardboard, a spring, and a black string that Claudia pulled at the appropriate time. Then they looked at each other and William blurted out, "And what in hell was that all about? Jesus! We had a plan! You two could have at least let Grace and me in on it. I'm guessing Claudia had a bag of stuff under her smock, and opened it to make the smells, but what was this Mrs. Modell thing? I thought we had it all set up. Sarah Joy must have told you about that hat's owner before."

Then William started to think. *No, that can't be it. Gary hadn't been in the basement before, so why would he know whose hat it was?* William had randomly picked the hat that he had attached to his hat launcher.

Claudia said, "I don't know where the smells came from, William," and quickly got in the car.

He turned to Gary, who said, "You guys aren't playing with me, are you? I talked tonight? I said I was someone named Michael?" Gary's eyes begged William to tell him it was a joke. No such explanation came. Gary got in the car and sped off down the road.

When William came back in, Sarah Joy was waiting for him, and Grace. She said, "You have a lot of explaining to do tomorrow. This wasn't funny." Then she smacked their bottoms and shooed them away so she could clean up.

Millie got a phone call in her car and so was the last to leave the parking lot. If she had looked into the ice cream shop that she passed, about a mile away, she might have noticed Gary and Claudia as they sat and split a banana split, laughing with each other.

(Only read on if you want to know more.)

Ending (continued). At the very end of the night, Sarah Joy watched Millie's Jeep until it was well down the road. Sarah Joy then swept the premises (*cop talk*) to make certain that Millie had left nothing behind—so she would not be back in a few minutes for her glasses or anything. Sarah Joy got a small gift box out from behind the counter. She nestled the bullet snugly among four cotton squares and lovingly but cautiously buried it in the back yard, using the flashlight she had last used when she had bought her salon. It was an interesting little gift, but Sarah Joy didn't want it anywhere in the salon. There was no way to dispose of it, so burial seemed to make sense.

Ending (continued). The next day, Claudia put a yearbook in an envelope and sent it back to a school in Minnesota—the high school from which Sarah Joy had graduated. It was from Sarah Joy's senior year. It's amazing how much information you can get from one of these things, if you're lucky, take a few minutes to prepare, and do your homework.

Ending (continued). The next evening, when Gary came home for dinner, Claudia got serious at the dinner table.

"Do you think what we did was too creepy for Sarah Joy?" Claudia said. "We were lucky to figure out the story of Mrs. Modell."

"I thought we did that rather well! A good research job," Gary said.

"But that hat, Gary," Claudia said. What are the odds that Sarah Joy would have had one of her hats, and that it would have been in the basement, and that William would have picked it as *the* hat?"

"Claudia," Gary said, "I've been shaking all day. We had it all planned out, but to be honest, I remember sitting down, remember asking if anyone wanted some more wine, then was surprised when people told me what I had just done."

"You did just what we planned!" Claudia said.

"But I don't remember doing any of it. And what scared me more was some comment about me/Michael having some kind of accent. I wouldn't have even thought to do such a thing," Gary admitted.

The rest of dinner was eaten in silence. Perhaps it was a very, very long pause. Dead air.

Ending (continued). That night, two people we know went to bed smiling. Gary was smiling because, of course, he remembered all that he did, and thought he did a good job on the little accent. Sarah Joy was smiling (different bed), proud of herself for telling a little white lie, that the hat that had "jumped" off the wall belonged to Grandma M. She really had no idea whose it was, that's why it was in the basement.

Also, she probably won't ever mention that the librarian at her old high school, also known to Sarah Joy as Aunt Fran, did alert her that someone has specifically asked to borrow a copy of the yearbook from the year Sarah Joy graduated, because they were planning a "special surprise for her".

- 12 -

STALKER LADY||LOVERBOY

The car was far enough away that Sarah Joy couldn't actually make eye contact with the woman sitting behind the wheel, but a periodic right hand passing through the long, dark hair caught her attention. After sitting in the lot for an hour, seemingly staring at the shop and only staring at the shop, the driver decided to pull out just as Sarah Joy was putting on her coat to confront the visitor. Sarah Joy had never expected her place to be cased by a woman, much less at 3:00 on a Monday afternoon.

At two o'clock on Tuesday afternoon, the car was back. Sarah Joy tried to be positive. It could be a million things—maybe a mother who drops off her child for dance class four blocks away, and is looking for a spot to just sit and park and wait to pick the child up. But here she was again. At 2:45 PM, the woman in the car got out and slowly walked into The Conscilience.

Grace, knowing that Sarah Joy was anxious over their observer, decided she'd make initial contact.

"Hi," Grace beamed. "Welcome to The Conscilience. What can I do for you?"

"Is this your place?" the visitor asked.

"No, my name's Grace. The owner is with a customer at the moment. What can I help you with?"

The visitor cheerily said, "You can tell her to either come out here or I'll go in there—that's what you can do for me."

"OK ... And your name is?"

All Grace got back was a cold stare. Well, chilly. Really chilly.

Now Grace is all about happiness, simplicity, and balance, but she's also no pushover.

I asked you a question, bitch, she didn't say.

"Your name?" she asked again, as if it were for the first time.

"I told you I want her out here, honey," Miss Pleasant flatly stated. "I've got a short fuse and I'm through with you. It's your move."

Grace pulled out a Grace Pause. It crumbled at these low temperatures.

"Let me *see* if she can break away for a moment," Grace said, and as she moved to Sarah Joy's styling room, she passed the basement door, reached in and pulled a purple fly swatter off a hook on the door. She threw it down the steps.

Almost a year ago, after a creepy guy roamed in and didn't seem to want to leave, they all sat down and talked about "signs" to use that would mean something was wrong. They developed a short three-burst wave (that's what they called it; you can create your own visual). They identified a rarely used word, "peacock," that would be worked into a sentence to signal trouble. And they identified a signal prop: a purple flyswatter, one of four around the shop. The swatters blend nicely into the walls.

Grace said quietly to Sarah Joy, who was fluffing Mrs. Ford's hair, "You'd better come out—crazy stalker lady is here to see you and only you."

At the same time, William thought he heard a "snap" in the basement—something had hit something. Weird! Oh, well, back to his phone call. And so the purple flyswatter sat on the fifth step, unable to talk, unable to elaborate on her presence. This is one of the most common frustrations of being a purple flyswatter. Another is picking on small bugs who don't deserve to die so young. William also couldn't hear the voices upstairs.

"Hello, welcome to The Conscilience," Sarah Joy said, extending her hand. "How can I help you?"

"You can follow a simple little rule for me. Only five words long. Words to live by. 'Keep away from my husband.'"

With that, she turned and walked away.

Sarah Joy caught the door before it closed. "Wait? Can't you talk to me?" she yelled. "I don't even know who you are!"

"Just think about it, honey. If you can't figure it out, hopefully you can at least get down to a few possibilities. Christ, how many husbands you got poking you?" the woman bleated back while still moving. Then she hastily slid into her car and was gone.

Sarah Joy went through a mental inventory. The woman was thin, with long black hair. She wore a black knit dress, white crocheted sweater that was loosely slung across her shoulders, and lots of silver—two silver rings, two silver necklaces, two silver bracelets on each arm. The nouveau-hippy-with-an-attitude look. Whenever a husband came for a haircut, Sarah Joy found a way to get a spousal description. None were close.

Sarah Joy knew she had nothing to worry about, but perhaps one of her gentlemen clients did have a crush on her of which she was unaware. It made her nervous. So did the next guy she met.

William had been curious since his first day why there wasn't a man (or a woman) in Sarah Joy's life. After watching for a while, he felt that this was a decision made consciously by her. If one watched Sarah Joy long enough, one might believe that having a relationship with a man just wasn't going to happen for her. When the opportunity arises, she always pushes them away.

"So the painter asked me out," she told William after he spent the day at The Conscilience touching up some of the white woodwork.

"Did you say yes?" William asked. "Let me guess. No." He knew what the answer was.

"I said no," she confirmed.

"Why do you always do that?" William asked her, suddenly feeling like this was a very inappropriate boss/worker conversation.

"I just don't find anything attractive in him," she said, trying to trivialize it.

"Nothing at all?" William asked. "Who cares? Just go out with him to see what it's like! It's good practice."

She just shrugged it off, like she does every time. Well, almost every time.

When Bob called, he said that Laurie had spoken highly of Sarah Joy. He had recently gotten out of the hospital and wanted to treat himself by finding a good place to get his hair cut. When he walked through the front door that afternoon, it wasn't a Sarah Joy Pause that filled the room as much as an unabashed ogle. Tall and well-constructed, with a fine, exquisitely trimmed beard, he was definitely politician material. He wore a grey suit, no tie, and the softest silk shirt. As he filled out his "client info" card, Sarah Joy looked at the one thing that is a turn-on/off for her—neck hair. How can men neglect their hairline in the back just because they can't see it? She glanced at him—a side view—and OMFG, he had a chiseled hairline across the back of his neck, exactly at the collar line. And he was here for a *haircut*? She silently gushed, in more ways than one. During a short tour of the salon, Bob stayed close, frequently so close that their arms touched. In Sarah Joy's styling room, he stood straight and still, in a very relaxed way, like it was natural. He let Sarah Joy remove his jacket and hang it up.

Now, if a man wants to make points with a woman, they can be a good listener. Bob uses a different approach—he does all of the talking and tells stories that make women adore him. He knows his stories are good ones.

"So, Bob, you said on the phone you were recently in the hospital?" Sarah Joy said, looking into his eyes.

"Second time," Bob said. "It's been a crazy few years. A friend of mine put me in the hospital—almost killed me."

(*Has good friends, was almost killed—what an intriguing guy!*)

Bob hoped it was working.

"Three years ago," Bob continued, "I was driving down Van Nuys Street in a restored 1967 Chevrolet Impala Super Sport. I had just bought it three weeks before—the first time I had ever saved up and paid cash, so I would never have to make a payment. I was feeling good. I never saw her car. She had a stroke and blacked out about half a block before the intersection. She never knew that her car slammed directly into mine—like I had a target painted on the driver's-side door. Her car broke all of my left ribs, punctured a lung, and sliced my liver in half, and my right knee hit the dash and ripped open. From the outside I looked almost untouched, since most of the injuries were internal. Technically, I was DOA at the hospital, but they easily revived me. The people at University Hospital were wonderful. Except for my knee, they fixed me up good as new. My father took two pictures of my car—from the right side, it was my baby. From the other side—ugh! I couldn't look at it.

"Recently, I was at a birthday party," he continued. A good buddy of mine—good, but not an old friend—was roughhousing. He picked me up and gave me a bear hug. 'You're so skinny I could break you in half,' he joked.

"I begged him to stop," Bob said, "as I was in the process of passing out from the pain. Typical of this guy, he didn't notice I was in pain, so he laughed, shaking me around like a rag doll.

"That evening, I noticed my abdomen had swelled a bit, and over the next few days it got bigger and hurt much more. I said, 'Get me to the emergency room.'

"Apparently I had some internal damage that the doctors hadn't detected earlier. My friend's little love squeeze ruptured some stressed parts of my intestines. I suppose it would have happened eventually, even if I hadn't been mauled."

As the story was told, Bob oh-so-casually unbuckled his pants—unbutton, unzip. Up goes his shirt with one hand and down go his boxers (about halfway) with the other.

"They had to get in here fast," he said pointing to his scar. The scar itself wasn't a pretty one to Sarah Joy, but his belly was. His skin was. His clothes were half off, and he was just so casual, so cavalier.

(Incidentally, so was the car that hit him. A Cavalier. 1983. A curious and useless fact is that Sarah Joy had also owned one. She always called it her crappymobile, another useless fact.)

Sarah Joy wasn't thinking about cars, but concerning the body before her, she wasn't protesting. She knew they'd moved from PG to R in this little play.

"Well, let's see if we can keep hair out of there." Sarah Joy smiled. She provided that as an excuse to put Bob back together before the staff saw whatever was happening. She was sure something in his boxers moved, and she realized she had to cool off—to continue the flirtation while getting to a safer place. Sarah Joy smoothed Bob's shirt down, zipped up his pants and buckled his belt. Clearly, Bob enjoyed the attention. Sarah Joy was watching herself, thinking that she would never zip up a guy's pants and buckle his belt. She decided it was OK, since there is more than one Sarah Joy. This one, the sexual one, was eager to spend some time out in the fresh air, although her desires pushed her brain and body awkwardly. She quickly got his hair washed, got him into a smock/gown, and enjoyed a delightful conversation as she trimmed a perfectly fine haircut on a perfectly fine head.

When Sarah Joy finished up, she said, "So, Bob, would you like me to brush those little cut hairs off your shirt, or would you like to be reminded of me all day?" It was a line she often used in her semi-flirt with male clients, but this time it came out very seriously.

"Reminded, definitely," he said, as he touched her arm. Bob got up out of the chair and headed to reclaim his jacket from its hanger in the closet. Of course, between chair and closet stood Sarah Joy. She dodged left, as did he, and they softly collided.

"Thank you. You did a wonderful job," he said as he was close to her, looking in her eyes. Then he kissed her. Light and playful, not serious, not such a big deal that one could protest in an adult world. The second was a little more serious.

Sarah Joy's life is largely about control. She seems to do whatever is necessary so that she has maximum control all of the time. But at that moment, control was placed on a glass shelf as Sarah Joy allowed the other Sarah Joy to enjoy the moment. She and Bob stood in the styling room for about five minutes, kissing.

Yes. Kissing. Making out like teenagers. Scandalous!

When William opened the front door with his McDonald's bag and shake, a flushed Sarah Joy led Bob to the desk.

"See you in six weeks?" she asked, as they stood close, looking into a schedule book. It wasn't even open to the right month. Neither noticed.

"I'll call," Bob said. "Sometimes my schedule is crazy. I'm not sure what it will be like six weeks from now yet."

And out he went. Sarah Joy's urge to pat his bottom was painfully strong, but it couldn't happen with William there.

Wow, that was nice. He was nice. The poor thing—he's been through so much. His story had friends, a birthday party, and a father in it, she pondered. *He was in an accident and alcohol wasn't involved. It was all so good.*

Still, something just wasn't right. Was it Sarah Joy looking for an excuse to protect herself from the uncontrollable parts of life? Whatever wasn't right, maybe it was just some minor imperfection that could be overlooked. She hoped.

That night, when Sarah Joy climbed the stairs and sat on her bed, she finally had time to think through the Bob visit.

What was wrong?

She tried to replay every second with Bob again.

Stop thinking about the kiss! she had to keep saying to herself. She then remembered *that* part of his story: "I said, 'Get me to the emergency room.'" *Who did he say that to?*

Sarah Joy tried hard to glide back down the steps. She was practicing—*glide like you're coming down without purpose, not in a rush. Glide. Be relaxed.* But it was not an elegant thing. She snapped up Bob's information card, which she had left on the counter. Yes, the "married" box was checked. She had purchased some software to more efficiently run the salon, and Sarah Joy put all client information in it, but she didn't spend time learning how to use it. She poked around in the program, and eventually found, in a pulldown menu, "search"; under that, one choice was "phone number." She punched in Bob's number and hit the search button. She didn't type in the smiley face he drew after his phone number. It was a good hunch. Laurie's number came up. Laurie's and Bob's were the same. *I suppose one could say he made it clear that he was married to Laurie.* Didn't he tell Sarah Joy? Laurie had told Bob to go to Sarah Joy's. He had told Sarah Joy that. He had played it carefully. And Sarah Joy had kissed a client's husband. Not good.

Lying in bed that night, Sarah Joy had two things on her mind. One, of course, was Bob and Laurie. Thinking back, Laurie had never said much during her haircuts about her husband, except that she found him tiring at times. She had never even mentioned his name. Perhaps the marriage was on the rocks. Even so, Sarah Joy had to back off. She was *almost* relieved that she had found a reason to avoid a male whom she found attractive, and so it was.

The second thing on her mind was Halloween. What a great day! Maybe it was a pivotal point in the relationship between Alicia and The Conscilience. Millie was now a client, so they'd see each other more. The séance was, well, whatever it was. What bothered her a bit was that Alicia's mother had called to thank her for sending her daughter home in such a good mood, and with presents.

"Did she rob the place or something?" Susan laughed, followed by a quick, "Keep up the good work, Sarah Joy," and her signature dial tone.

Something didn't fit. Susan had called and asked Sarah Joy to make some royal room because the former Miss America needed attention *now*. Alicia was so excited for the personal message and photo from Calluna. It just seemed strange that, in the time Susan spent covering Calluna's visit to town, she would not have mentioned her own hearing-impaired daughter, Alicia. When Sarah Joy told Calluna about this deaf teen girl she knew, she expected Calluna to say, "Oh, Susan's daughter?" All strange. Perhaps Susan knew something about Calluna that she didn't want to talk about. Maybe she knew enough about Calluna that *she* didn't *want* her to meet her daughter. As her mind rolled it all over and inside out, one of her true loves, Mr. Sandman, slid into bed with her, and quickly took charge.

Zzzzzzzzzzz.

- 13 -

ANOTHER SATURDAY NIGHT

Sarah Joy's immediate problem with Bob was that the kissy-face game was on a Tuesday afternoon, and that week ended with not just a Saturday, but one that included *a* Saturday Night. Of course, for the first time, two of the attendees were "Laurie and spouse." Laurie and spouse, Suzy and Ralph, and Sarah Joy.

Sarah Joy's real Bob problem was with herself. She knew that she needed to do the right thing. One alternative was to sit Bob down and say "no more." An easier approach was to just cool it, and not have another day like the last one with him. She was purposely not giving it the time it deserved, and was feeling guilty that she didn't feel bad about Bob. Laurie is not exactly Sarah Joy's best friend or client, and can be just nasty at times. Perhaps this was all the beginning of an impending divorce. Why couldn't Sarah Joy think about a divorced man, if she liked him? She had to admit it would always be awkward for Laurie, but if Laurie decided to go elsewhere, it would increase Sarah Joy's "nice client" quotient to 98.4 percent! Sarah Joy chose to not think this through for now.

After Suzy and Ralph arrived (late), they were introduced to Bob and Laurie. While waiting for Sarah Joy to roll some chairs into her salon room Laurie, quickly bored, asked how these two obvious characters met.

"Oh, it was just a day in the city," Suzy said. "Ralph was in line for a slice of pizza at Ray-Ray's. I was doing a little sightseeing and saw the line at Ray's, which told me their pizza was good. I was hungry, and got in line behind Ralph.

"So, he got up to the counter and said 'A slice of pepperoni, and put it in the oven,'" Suzy explained. "The guy said 'It's hot.' Ralph said, 'I like to burn my mouth. Put it in the oven.' The counter guy looked a little more disgusted. 'It's hot,' he said again. Ralph said, 'I've been standing in line looking at this slice of pizza for five minutes. You pizza guy. Me customer. *Put it in the oven!*'"

Suzy finally took a breath (the sign of a professional talker.)

"It wasn't a big thing," Ralph jumped in. "You just gotta know how to deal with these guys."

"I thought they were going to hit each other," Suzy jumped back in.

"Women! I wasn't mad at him. He wasn't mad at me. I was buying a slice of pizza," Ralph yelled, because that was how he talked.

"You were yelling at each other," she tried to explain, "just like you are yelling now."

"Yelling—Christ, you *still* don't know nothin'." Ralph turned to Suzy.

"Now *you're* yelling at *me*," Suzy pointed out, then turned to Laurie. "Ain't he yelling at me?"

"Good thing you ain't selling pizza, honey. You'd be broke," Ralph yelled at Suzy. He then surprised Bob by jumping up, running over to Suzy and grabbing her. Bob wondered if he should protect her; Laurie just watched.

Ralph started tickling Suzy, who was soon yelling as well—yelling and giggling.

This was Ralph and Suzy's life. To Suzy, it seemed like he was always hollering, but he was never mad. It always kept her off-balance, but she loved him and he was fun. Ralph, of course, "didn't see nothin' wrong."

"She's just quiet, that's all," Ralph explained to Bob and Laurie. "Whatchagonnado?"

Ralph was refreshing; you always knew exactly what you were getting with him. You could just look at him, and his disheveled black hair told you so. With Suzy, it was a different matter. No one knew Suzy; not well. She was "nice" and gentle and dependable, but clearly/probably had dimensions she wasn't showing.

When Sarah Joy broke out the eats and wine and joined them, both men perked up. "What, no pizza?" Ralph grinned.

Bob got up every time Sarah Joy entered the room. It wasn't clear why—maybe to help her (but he didn't), maybe to pick up a food tray and serve people (he didn't). He just was good at somehow semi-pacing, but always being close to Sarah Joy—her little shadow.

Sarah Joy is slowly learning to over-organize activities. She is not about to ever be associated with a dull time, so whenever a group is present, she almost always thinks up things to do well in advance. At her best, she pulls out a fun game just when conversation slows. If her idea is bad, people play and hope it will be over. Most often, her idea of fun delights everyone. Bob's wife, Laurie, just isn't a game person. Whenever a game is announced, she groans. Games make her feel stupid and look stupid, she has correctly realized. (She's pointed this out once to Bob, but he was watching *Jeopardy* and didn't respond.)

Sarah Joy was excited about the plan tonight. She'd invented a game recently and was beta-testing. She introduced it as *Sarah Joy's Connections*. (Everyone got the joke. A local budget hair-cuttery is called *Connections*. It doesn't make sense, but it's what their neon sign says. Our best guess is that they bought the sign from a singles bar that folded up somewhere.)

The rules of *Sarah Joy's Connections* are easy to follow. Each person is handed three pieces of light purple paper on which they write down three words, one on each paper. They are then thrown into an old lady hat (the pieces of paper, not the people). In a second hat, each person's name is on a little piece of paper. A player is selected from that hat, and they then pick three words from the other. With the words, they have to make a connection, in the order in which they were pulled (a rule that few follow). You can succeed by being either really smart or really creative. Succeed and you get a marble. Fail and you help wash dishes or sweep up, Sarah Joy threatens.

While cutting Laurie's hair that night, Sarah Joy had introduced the game and picked a name. She wished she hadn't picked Bob's name first, but she did. From the second hat, Bob selected three words.

"OK, let's see what I have to work with. Oh, wonderful: *elephants, billiard balls,* and *movies.*"

Bob was smart enough not to point out that *billiard balls* is two words.

Sarah Joy had tried this game with a few other groups; she noticed that she usually writes down animals or plants. Laurie wrote *swimming, TV,* and *drinking* (apparently things she'd rather be doing). Bob wrote things he'd rather be doing as well (go-go girls, Sarah Joy, billiard balls.)

As the mandatory snickering and yacking ended, Bob began. "Did you know that, right after the Civil War, Americans went crazy over billiards? They created such a demand for ivory that it almost drove elephants to extinction. In the 1860s, a billiard supplier offered a $10,000 prize for man-made ivory. A guy in Albany tried to make a fibrous goop that could be poured into molds."

"Bob, remember, you didn't get 'billiards.' You got 'billiard balls,'" Laurie reminded him.

"Well, what do you think I'm talking about?" he said, bordering on annoyed.

"I have no clue, but look—billiard balls, elephants, and movies. You gotta hit these three instead of beating around the elephant bush," she said, trying to look bored.

"I should either shoot you or shoot me, Laurie." Bob laughed. He wasn't smiling. "I'm trying to collect my thoughts. Let me be more explicit. *Billiard balls* were made of *ivory, which is elephant tusk. John Hyatt* tried to make a synthetic ivory. He molded *billiard balls* out of some goop he concocted. The problem was whenever the balls hit each other, they exploded. He never won the prize money, but his new invention made him a lot more.

"Do you know what it was?" he challenged the group.

Laurie, definitely not knowing when to quit, tried to just say something nonsensical. "*Gone with the Wind?*" she asked.

187

"That's right, hon," Bob said. "Celluloid!"

If knowledge were a deep ocean, Laurie would be floating on or above the water. She said *Gone With the Wind* and they heard celluloid?

Must.

Drink.

More!

Ralph smiled and said, "Well, I'm impressed. So, is all of this true? How would we know whether or not you made up all of these things, Bob?"

"Next time I'll try to use more common connections, so the little people will understand," Bob smiled. Ralph snorted. At least Ralph was authentically enjoying this game!

Laurie chugged her thirty-fourth glass of Chablis, and started waving her arms, pretending like she had to desperately try to get someone's attention. "Oh, Bobbbbb! Yoohoo. Hellooooo. You still have 'movies'!

Now the group quickly realized that they might have to work around this side of Laurie, but this was getting uncomfortable for all of them. A Sarah Joy Pause filled them all like dead batteries in their iPods.

"Honey," Bob finally said, "celluloid is movie film."

"And did everybody know that?" Laurie asked, as she looked at each of them.

"Well, yes, I've heard references to celluloid concerning movies before," Suzy reluctantly answered.

"Huh!" was all Laurie could say.

Sarah Joy dove right in. "OK, great job, Bob. Let's see who's next."

Bob picked up the name hat, holding it over Sarah Joy's head. She reached up, picked a piece of paper, and announced "Me!" Bob, looking over her shoulder, saw that Sarah Joy had not, in fact, picked her own name, but Laurie's. Sarah Joy was not pleased that Bob had looked over her shoulder, further contributing to the Sarah Joy/Bob/Laurie complication.

Sarah Joy then picked three words from hat number two and read them aloud: "*Bunnies, flowers,* and *booze.*"

"We *do* need to fine tune this game," Sarah Joy admitted. "I could tell you that bunnies and flowers are on the cover of the first edition of *The Adventures of Peter Cottontail* (the book, Laurie, not *Cotton Petertail*, the porno movie), and whenever my father would read this book to me, he would drink booze when he was done, but that shouldn't be an acceptable connection. I could be making the part about my father up, and you couldn't confirm it. But if I said bunnies and flowers are on the cover of the first edition of *The Adventures of Peter Cottontail* by Thornton Burgess, who died from alcohol poisoning, that would be good! You could confirm it all on the Internet if someone challenged any of my information."

Everyone nodded. She was relieved that they didn't challenge her.

The next two names randomly picked were Bob (again) and Laurie. Bob selected *dictionary, mail,* and *insane.* He told the story of James Murray, William Minor, and the *Oxford English Dictionary,* which took thirty years to finish. In the 1870s Dr. Murray, the editor, asked the public for help. Dr. William Minor made many contributions by mail, submitting more than ten thousand definitions over a period of twenty years! For that time period, the two men corresponded often but never met. Eventually Murray learned that Minor had been convicted of murder and was being kept in an asylum, where he was classified as "criminally insane." It was from the asylum that Minor had submitted his many definitions.

Laurie rolled her eyes. Suzy actually was interested! Laurie asked if, at the end, she would have earned her GED since it was all "such *educational fun.*"

After Laurie's name was picked, Sarah Joy quickly selected three words for her, because it was clear she wasn't going to actually get up. According to Sarah Joy, Laurie's three words were *sweater, girl,* and *TV.* Again, Bob looked over her shoulder and knew which three words had really been selected. Laurie talked about a sit-com she had watched the previous night. Sarah Joy's idea was confirmed: if you take enough control, everyone could be happy!

Although it was a slightly awkward time, Sarah Joy was confident that *Connections* was entertainment worthy of development. With a little work, a few more rules, and maybe if she picked *all* of the words and thought more about the people involved, it could work. Having surprised herself in reading Laurie's name as her own, Sarah Joy knew that all would be OK, as long as she took charge of reading the words without anyone ever again looking over her shoulder.

And as quickly as it had begun, *Sarah Joy's Connections* hats were gone and the whirlwind called Sarah Joy carried the group to other, previously selected topics of conversation. She was so good and it all appeared to happen so naturally that Bob almost failed to be impressed. Ralph was surprised that not everyone even got a turn, but it was clear why.

Throughout the conversation, Sarah Joy watched Laurie. She had the reputation of getting dumber and louder when she drinks, but neither was true. She's a pretty girl. She does not exactly have a "China doll" look, to use what must now be considered a very non-PC phrase, but she has flawless skin, black hair (always pulled back, although she looks great when she lets it down), and stunning blue eyes. She doesn't look like someone who is in such a lifeless marriage. Bob and Laurie don't talk to each other much, but each can authentically be fun to be around.

While everyone in the group was yapping/yelling/talking, Sarah Joy's ears perked up a bit. To her it sounded like the front door. Maybe not. No one appeared—so it could be William or Grace. A moment later, she detected movement, out of range of her guests. Near the front door, she watched a coat being hung on one of the hooks by a hand, a woman's hand. On the hand was a silver ring—two! Slowly, her unexpected visitor appeared in the doorway. This time it wasn't 3:00 PM but 8:00 PM. The last time she was there, she had stood in The Conscilience ready to explode, almost ready to strangle Sarah Joy because of her husband. But who? Sarah Joy had a feeling she would finally get an answer to that question.

Sarah Joy jumped toward her. Before she knew it, she had a hand on the woman's shoulder as she gently stopped her forward motion.

"Well, uh, hello," Sarah Joy stuttered. "I don't want any trouble here." Realizing she was touching the woman, she pulled her hand quickly back. "Oh, I'm *so* sorry."

The visitor didn't budge. Sarah Joy had not observed before that this woman was actually several inches taller than herself. The woman scowled down at her, briefly looked at the room full of people, and stepped around Sarah Joy.

"Oh, people! Good," she said. "I'm very sorry to involve you in all this, but I need to cleanse my soul and that takes a public act."

"A while ago," she continued, addressing her audience, "I came in here and pushed my weight around because your ... hostess here ... was seeing my husband. Last week he finally proclaimed his love for her to me, packed his bags and moved off with her to San Antonio." She turned to address Sarah Joy. "But it appears that *you* are here ... so it is highly likely at this point that his new love must own some other salon."

Sarah Joy nodded.

Stalker Lady frowned. "I'm Betsy. Betsy Thomas. I was very wrong. I feel like hell. Actually, losing Frederick was the easy part. I feel good about that now. But *you*—I was very nasty to you, and to the other woman who was here. So I want all of you to know that I was mean to this poor woman due to no fault of hers, and all I can say is that I'm not actually a bad person and I am very, very sorry. You deserved none of it. I'm an idiot. What can I say?"

Sarah Joy put her arm through the woman's arm and took her into another room.

"My name is Sarah. Sarah Joy. Thank you for coming back to tell me this. You've been an unresolved part of my life since we met. I've been waiting for the other shoe to fall."

"I am so sorry," Betsy repeated sincerely.

"Occasionally I have a late Saturday night when I cut some hair and have some wine and cheese and we talk." She gestured back toward the group. "Can I interest you in a glass of wine?" Sarah Joy asked, "and a trim?"

"You are very gracious and quite rightfully attempting to kill me with kindness, and yes, that does make me feel even more like crap. I've burned more than enough of your time and emotions. I need to go. Thanks again for being so understanding," Betsy said.

She reached hastily for her coat and her hand was met—stopped, actually, by another hand. A woman's hand. It was Laurie's. Betsy dropped her hand from the coat hook.

Laurie has this thing that she does. Only Bob had seen it before. She puts her two hands on her hips so that her elbows are pointing way back. This tends to push her breasts into a very prominent position—like a peacock spreading its feathers to say, "Don't mess with me," like a buck showing its rack, ready to rumble.

"While you two have been out *here*, we've been talking in *there*," Laurie explained. "You may be finished with us, Betsy, but we're not finished with you."

The two looked into each other's eyes. Both had on their most serious faces. Betsy was led back into the room filled with people who were strangers to her. She smiled, hoping she wouldn't get beaten too badly.

"We've made a decision," spokesperson Laurie continued. "In the chair, that's Ralph. He's with Suzy over there. His hair is almost done, and if it weren't, no one would really notice. After him, you're next. Sarah Joy will just have to work a little later tonight."

Laurie finished the introductions.

"Haven't I seen all of you people stuffing money into red kettles at Christmas or helping old ladies across the street or giving warm coats to homeless people?" Betsy asked.

"All this and sarcasm too!" Laurie actually perked up for the first time that night. "This is good. We value smart people who know how to verbalize their emotions." The line surprised everyone, but no one commented—she was on a roll!

"We're not quite ready to let you get away, Betsy. You just may have potential," Suzy said.

Wha? These people are a frisky bunch! Betsy didn't say.

And so it went. Names were exchanged for a second time, points in common were identified. By the end of the evening, each woman hugged Betsy, so both men took the opportunity to do so as well. Betsy took one of Grace's cards and sent her a small bouquet of flowers the next day.

Betsy has been a regular ever since, and has even gotten together with Suzy twice for lunch. They tried to fix her up with one of Ralph's friends from work, and Betsy was unusually gracious, but just wasn't ready to have to "deal with men" again, except for Bob and Ralph, with whom she has become very comfortable. Whenever she gets a little too sarcastic or picks on someone too much, they've learned to come up with loving little lines; their current choice is "tone it down, (b/w)itch!" It always makes her smile, and makes her plop down in the nearest chair, and practice five minutes of restraint and silence. OK, two minutes of restraint and silence. Actually, it's just an extended pause, but a very noticeable one. Pauses always find a good home in The Conscilience.

Betsy never got around to telling Sarah Joy that she also became pretty sure she had the wrong person when a bubbly, sweet woman at work, Jane Hamilton, happened to mention that she got her hair cut at The Conscilience. After hearing Jane gush over Sarah Joy, Betsy had to question her suspicions. It's too bad that conversation never happened. Sarah Joy would have heard of a side of Jane that she never could have imagined. Bubbly?

- 14 -

THE END
Thanks to each and every one of you
for stopping by

It is a Saturday night of course—the last Saturday night in January. Two couples are back: Bob and Laurie again, and Suzy and Ralph again. Bob and Sarah Joy now behave like a typical client/stylist pair, and Sarah Joy didn't have to do anything to fix it. When Bob found out that Laurie was likely sleeping around, instead of celebrating the possibility of being single in the near future, he instead cleaned up his part-time playboy act, asked Laurie if they could renew their vows, and the two of them are deep into their post-seven-year-itch love fest.

Millie and Miss Florrie also accepted invitations to play. Sarah Joy is so happy that her two girlfriends are joining the Saturday night group! For tonight, Sarah Joy— realizing how obsessed she'd become with trying to plan dozens of options to guarantee good evenings—forced herself to plan *nothing* except, of course, the food. She just felt so comfortable with Millie and Miss Florrie's endless pool of stories that the evening could surely take care of itself.

Everyone was already in Sarah Joy's styling room, and it promised to be an interesting evening. Bob and Laurie both just seemed to be different—more talkative, more interactive. Sarah Joy was so happy. Most of the time Bob was trying to catch Sarah Joy's attention with a please-forgive-me smile. Millie and Laurie seemed to be smiling at each other a little more. Ralph was a little louder than usual, having gotten a head start on the alcohol for the evening. For some reason, everyone decided to take their shoes off, so a line of shoes was against the wall. Discreetly in Millie's boot was her little concealed friend. Miss Florrie was the only holdout, suggesting that it was barbaric for a lady to show her naked feet to strangers. Miss Florrie's hat was on its hook, and her cane was standing up in one corner. Food and drink were flowing as usual, and Miss Florrie was first in the chair, fascinating everyone as they watched her getting her head shaved. She loves the attention. She's a rock star.

Ralph and his mild buzz decided to adopt Miss Florrie for the night. Associating old age with being hard-of-hearing, he sat down in a chair in front of her so she could hear him. Miss Florrie was getting quite a kick out of Ralph, Suzie and Millie, but wasn't sure what to make of the other two in the room. Somehow Miss Florrie and Ralph clicked when it came to weird topics of conversation, and everyone ended up listening to Ralph telling her about one of his get-rich-quick schemes.

"So I was flying home," Ralph told her. "Sometimes I have to travel for work, and I started talking to this guy on the plane. We were both pissed off about the same things. When you travel, you realize how precious your time is. So when people waste your time, you get pissed, right?"

He just said "pissed," Miss Florrie said to herself. I wonder if he knows what "sucks" means. They seem to be bundled so often.

Ralph continued. "We both had similar experiences. Got in late to hotels on our trip—no one at the front desk. We had to wake up some college kid sleeping in the back. On my last trip I wanted an iron and ironing board to iron my shirt. They couldn't find one, and it was too late to call around. There was a meeting at the hotel, which finished up just before I was ready to leave. So two hundred people wanted to check out at the same time. I missed my plane. My seatmate had many similar experiences. We decided we'd invent a chain of hotels dedicated to speed. Check in fast; check out fast; never have the process eat up your time. He thought he could even find some investors. We traded names and numbers. We even came up with a name: 'Inn-N-Out.'"

"Ralph, that's not even funny," Suzy said.

"It's not supposed to be funny—it says it all: fast, fast, fast," he said seriously.

"It says that you can rent rooms by the hour, bonehead!" Suzy laughed.

It would have been an even better story if Miss Florrie had spit her drink onto the nearby mirror, but she didn't. However, some did come out of her nose as she laughed—a look she definitely wasn't proud of. Nothing ever comes out of a lady's nose, you know.

All Ralph could come up with was "Huh?" It was Miss Florrie who actually took the time to explain the problems with the name to him. Everyone was surprised that this relationship had grown into a loving one. These three just couldn't seem to get enough of each other. (Miss Florrie had even showed up at a softball game that Ralph and Suzy's team played in one Sunday afternoon!)

The room was unusually loud as the group just enjoyed each other, and the happier they are, the more they eat. Miss Florrie kept playing with Ralph. She'd sit there with her mouth open until he noticed, and then he'd run and get a shrimp for her. Silly kids.

Millie was sitting on a short footstool waiting for her turn for a trim. For much of that time, Laurie had been standing behind her, leaning against the doorjamb. Millie enjoyed sitting down low; she could keep her drink and plate of cheese and crackers on the floor in front of her. Laurie had noticed that, as Millie bent over, her short blue sweater rode up her back and her pants moved down to reveal a Victoria's Secret label on her thong. At this point, Laurie moved over behind her to have that view for the rest of the evening. No one thought anything of it, although the men certainly would have noticed this flash of white, fresh, young skin.

They drank; Laurie watched. Sarah Joy brought in three more bottles of wine and opened them to allow the wine to breathe. Millie, finding herself full of alcohol, slipped into the restroom. As she pulled the door behind her, it resisted for the last inch before it closed, then opened back up as Laurie slipped in and closed the door behind her. The two women faced each other, Laurie obviously wanting something, but not sure how to act. Millie had never been this close to Laurie. Millie couldn't help but look into her gorgeous eyes. Laurie touched Millie's hips with both hands and in a single motion brought their lips together—just a short kiss. Millie's heart raced. This was not something she had ever done before, but Laurie was in fact such a beautiful person, so soft to kiss, and so in control of the moment. They kissed again. This time, Millie did what at the time seemed very natural to do, pulling Laurie closer so that they touched from knees to lips. They hugged and Laurie slipped out, smoothly snagging Suzy, who was walking by, with one hand and closing the door with the other. No one had noticed.

It all left Millie very aroused. It was a warm and cozy thing for her, like being in her parents' living room on Thanksgiving with a fire in the fireplace. It felt very nice.

She wasn't sure how she would feel about what might happen next in a relationship like this. She was very fond of men and always had been, but one cannot work in a lab without feeling an obligation to, at times, experiment.

Still standing, a bit in shock, in the middle of this small bathroom, her eyes found the black-and-white picture on the wall of two old women sitting on a beach with their hats colorized purple. Below the picture, some words were typed on a small piece of paper. No client had ever actually read the photo caption before, although it had been on the bathroom wall for some time. Millie leaned closer and, whispering to herself, read the words:

As they woke up in the sand that morning

after the Flag Day party,

wondering what they had done the night before,

they at least felt good realizing that

they still had their bonnets on.

Millie slipped back into the group, a move noticed only by Miss Florrie. She sat in the hair-washing chair and waited until Sarah Joy was ready to start on her next head.

Ten minutes later, everyone was listening to a disembodied Millie story and didn't hear the front door open. Only Sarah Joy and Millie noticed the business end of a shotgun coming through the doorway into Sarah Joy's styling room. Sarah Joy raised her hand and everyone, responding to the look on her face, froze. The shotgun was followed into the room by the former Miss America, who walked up to Sarah Joy and stuck the barrel against her forehead.

"I know you," said Miss Florrie. "Didn't you used to be somebody?"

But Calluna didn't hear, and the one interpreter didn't look like he was on the job. With a rope around his neck, he was being dragged along behind her, and he clearly wasn't happy. She wasn't exactly dragging him along as a hostage, but she had already done enough persuading so that he was doing what she wanted without argument, at least for the moment.

"I'm so sorry," he said to Sarah Joy, when Calluna wasn't looking at him. "She falls into that 'not well-adjusted' category that you'd talked about," he explained.

Calluna saw his lips move and smacked him in the mouth with the gunstock. He started to bleed, through the fingers holding his mouth, onto the floor. Why she brought him at all was unclear, but it was carefully planned. The rope around his neck was held with a slipknot; one tug and the line around his neck would tighten. She had clearly passed a personal point of no return. In her best attempt at speaking directly, she explained that when she was in the salon before, she had asked for gum to be removed from her hair. She had assumed that a professional could do this without touching scissors. She had never asked that her bangs be trimmed.

"My bangs are the most important part of a close-up. They're not something you can just trim! I have a person who does that, and who knows more than you do. I looked so stupid that day, and the next day, and the next day, because of you, Sarah Joy. Hundreds of photos are taken of me every day. Don't you understand that? So I was very happy that I had this opportunity to, in my busy schedule, pass through town here today to properly thank you, you stupid bitch."

Sarah Joy asked her to let the others leave. Miss America made a strange sound that might have been laughter. She was a good lip reader.

"Let's just make sure you don't screw up anyone else, OK?" she said as she looked down the sight of the shotgun, preparing to blow Sarah Joy's head off. She had such a crazed look in her eyes—not Miss America material at all. She looked down the barrel and into Sarah Joy's eyes.

Bob, whom you might have thought would be first to act, did nothing, but he knew that something needed to be done, and soon. He was puzzled that no one was helping Sarah Joy. Laurie just found the whole thing curious. Ralph looked at Millie. She was, after all, the forensic scientist. She should know what to do. Unfortunately, lab workers rarely get instructed to perform as police officers. She had no training to prepare her for this.

Calluna's trigger finger moved onto the trigger, as trigger fingers are known to do. Her totally pissed-off look changed to a look of surprise as glass shattered on the top of her head, cutting her pretty little face as it followed the accompanying picture frame that quickly moved till it stopped on her shoulders. It was a most curious thing to see. The blood oozing from dozens of cuts held onto the back of her head a photograph of how she *used to* look.

Alicia, who had walked in unannounced, was delighted to find her hearing impaired hero, shocked that she had a shotgun, and decided that having a weapon aimed at Sarah Joy was generally unacceptable.

"Here's your picture back, you creep," Alicia said as she smashed the frame, complete with a signed black-and-white, over Calluna's head. It felt like she had been building up sixteen years of anger and frustration just to let it all go, at this second, in one swing that would let her start her life over.

As Miss America was realizing that her life as a beauty queen was probably history, the shotgun started to fall from her hand, discharging in the process, firing into the stockroom. Everyone, particularly the screaming Calluna, was a bit surprised to watch Alicia pick up the shotgun and use the gunstock to break a piece of glass that was held by blood onto Calluna's forehead. The force of the gunstock took Calluna down, where she stayed until the ambulance came for Miss America, and, unfortunately, the police for Alicia.

The group was also surprised when Alicia calmly ejected the shell from the shotgun, which was still smoking, and dropped it into Miss Florrie's wine glass. She would later explain that one of her favorite daddy-daughter activities was hunting, so she knew her way around a gun.

While they waited, Alicia calmly explained that she had been bragging to one of her deaf friends about her personally signed photo from Miss America, and her girlfriend had one too! Same photo, same personally signed message, even the same spider story! She decided to just give it back to Sarah Joy with a message for Calluna to shove it. She was happy to have shown up at the right time and do what needed to be done to stop the shooting attempt.

The police left with Alicia after getting statements from everyone there. The officer assured them all that Alicia had to be taken in for prints, but it was clearly an act of self defense. She had stopped a crime from happening. She had likely saved the lives of everyone in the room, and she would surely be released. She might even get some kind of hero's award from the mayor before it was all over. They said they'd make sure someone brought her back for her car. We'll never know if Sarah Joy's decision to tell the police who Alicia's parents were helped them decide how to treat her, but they were gentle and understanding, and explained to her what they were doing and why. Alicia could only think that this put her in the same badass category as Millie.

Saturday Night at Sarah Joy's, Bob thought. *Bring something to pass, come hungry and thirsty, and don't forget your flack jacket!*

As the group marveled over Alicia's ability to calmly save the day and satisfy her feelings of anger and desire for revenge, Sarah Joy swept up the glass and broken frame. She kept the bloodstained photo. If Alicia didn't want it back, Sarah Joy intended to reframe it. Everyone was in the middle of a pretty good adrenaline rush, so they did what they did best. They kept talking. Miss Florrie, who was holding up very well, thought of the one word that kept puzzling her—*sucks*. The closest she could get was some reference to the word *vacuum*, and she couldn't imagine it was a reference to her vacuum cleaner at home. Miss Florrie decided that she was enjoying Ralph too much, and was ignoring Bob, so she turned to him. "Bob, you seem to be a very smart person. Could you explain something to me?"

"Certainly, if I can," he said, optimistic that he probably could.

"What does the word 'vacuum' mean?" she asked. "I'm sure it's something I know, but there must be something I'm missing."

"*Vacuum*? What do you mean?" Bob asked, not sure how to proceed.

"It's what *sucks* up dirt in the house, honey," piped up Laurie.

"Sucks" and "vacuum" used together. I must be on the right track, Miss Florrie thought.

"This room is full of air—little molecules bouncing around ..." Bob began. Then he explained getting rid of the molecules, leaving behind a low pressure, a vacuum. "Does that help?"

"Yes, dear, I suppose," Miss Florrie said, still a bit confused. "I've seen the word used in so many ways, I never appreciated what it meant."

"Well, it's not supposed to be a reference to what's in Laurie's head," Bob smiled.

"Oh, dear, that's certainly not why it popped into my mind. I've always found science facts interesting," Miss Florrie said, looking at Laurie, trying to explain.

Both Sarah Joy and Ralph said, simultaneously, "I've used a vacuum before."

"OK, Sarah Joy, ladies first," Ralph waved her on.

"Well, since we find it interesting to be so honest with each other, I can tell you a little secret. I have a little vacuum pump that was made to work on a woman's lips—anyone's lips, I suppose. You place the seal around your lips and pump out the air. It pulls extra blood into your lips and makes them fuller for a few hours. Sometimes when I'm feeling frisky, I'll make my lips a little fuller."

"God, the things women do," Bob said, becoming yet a little less interested in Sarah Joy. He could just picture kissing her and having her lips explode. *How do you get blood off a silk shirt?*

"That's really not good for you," Bob told her. "Small blood vessels on the surface of your skin can break. I guess on your lips you wouldn't notice, but I bet if you did it on your arm, you'd see red splotches."

"Break blood vessels?" Ralph anxiously asked. "What do you mean? A vacuum breaks blood vessels? That sounds bad, Bob."

"Well, Ralph, sounds like there is a story in you too," Bob smiled. "Spill."

"Now I feel even more stupid. Breaking blood vessels—Christ!" Ralph shook his head.

"Ralph, you don't need to tell them," Suzy said.

"Aww, come on, hon. If not here, where? These are my friends," Ralph said, always ready to embarrass himself. The alcohol was a good lubricant. "When I was in college, the fraternity decided to buy—sorry, Miss Florrie, no disrespect—a penis pump."

There was no pause. There was silence. No one would call this much time a pause. Uncomfortable with the silence, Ralph continued.

"It was $59.95. You somehow pumped it to suck extra blood into your penis by making a vacuum around it—in a tube with a pump. It was supposed to make your d—I mean, *thing*, bigger."

Suzy tried to get small and disappear into her chair. Miss Florrie, on the other hand, was just fascinated.

"Then you were supposed to slip a rubber ring around the, uh, base of your *thing*, to keep it, uh, inflated," Ralph's wine said.

Sarah Joy started to giggle. She wasn't in control of this one—it spilled out and filled the room. Only Miss Florrie had a serious look on her face—in the interest of science, of course.

"And big!" Suzy said. "This thing was amazing. Two inches became almost three."

"Oh, dear," said Miss Florrie. Laurie snorted. Millie snorted. They looked at each other and smiled.

"I'm sorry, Miss Florrie," Ralph said. "We don't mean nothin'. We're harmless."

"I was just wondering what my life would have been like if these vacuum pumps had been around when my husband, Horatio, was still alive," Miss Florrie said. She tried hard to create a cackle, having seen the word "cackle" often but not really knowing what it sounded like. Instead, she made a noise like a door creaking.

"Well, me and the boys, maybe we never read the instructions right or something, but I don't think it changed many lives," Ralph continued. "And we were too embarrassed to compare notes. We kept it in the upstairs hallway cabinet. First time it was gone, the bathroom door was closed. Next time, the bathroom door closed. We had to experiment with the thing, you know. Then one time, the pump was gone, Otto's door was closed, and a necktie was hanging on the doorknob. Otto and his sweetie, Shug, were putting the pump to the test. Then we heard Shug laughing. Just like Sarah Joy was laughing—just now. Then it was outta control laughing. It kept going. Christ, no guy can be romantic with a girl laughing like that. They left real soon and nobody wanted to try it out after that."

"Let me get this straight, Ralph," Bob said. "You all stuck your *things* into the same tube?"

"Oh, God—we washed it. We sterilized it like mad. Just the thought of who used it last could ruin you forever. You washed it for a few hours before you tried to use it.

We sorta had a pattern down. But anyway, what do you think, Bob? Did I blow out blood vessels with this thing?"

"I'm not a doctor, but I'm pretty sure you healed long ago," Bob assured him.

"After it was pumped up bigger than life, did you say, 'I'm the customer. You're the pizza girl. Just stick it in your hot oven?'" Laurie laughed, rolling onto the floor.

"You people know way too much," Ralph complained.

Bob sat his pressed suit pants down on Sarah Joy's styling chair to get his trim. Sarah Joy tried not to stare at his trimmed neckline, but it was difficult. There was a knock at the door. Everyone looked at each other.

"You can't be serious?" Miss Florrie said.

Millie offered to go see who it was, but stopped first to get her handgun out of her boot. She slipped it into her back pocket.

"Delivery guy!" she yelled as she opened the door, putting everyone at ease—that is everyone except Sarah Joy, who immediately detected the smell of a burning cigarette and knew that something was very wrong.

Millie walked back into Sarah Joy's styling room with a big FedEx uniform behind her. Between them was Millie's gun, firmly pressed against her back. In The Uniform's other hand was a much larger .357 Magnum. He puffed on the cigarette that was hanging off his lip, filling the room with a smoky haze.

He pushed Millie roughly down to the floor, against the wall, and looked around the room. There was food and open bottles of alcohol everywhere. "What a life. Barber pole ain't good enough for you pretty boys?" he scowled.

Ralph, who had had more than enough of this silliness, and more than enough Zinfandel, stood up and started to swagger toward The Uniform. The Uniform swung his big pistol through Ralph's head, and he hit the floor hard. Suzy screamed and dove for him. He was OK, clearly breathing, but that was a bad cut on his temple, and a now more blood appeared on Sarah Joy's once beautiful wood floor. The floor was definitely developing a character, not unlike how it looked the first time Sarah Joy and the floor had met.

The Uniform watched Suzy trying to care for Ralph, and Millie, who was just holding her head. "Can I get you broads' attention?" The Uniform barked. "Christ! I have a gun here! Thanks to stupid, I have two!"

The Uniform slid Millie's pistol under his belt so he could flick his cigarette ashes on the floor. He pointed his gun at the group as he talked.

"Now this here is what you call a simple, old-fashioned robbery," The Uniform said. From somewhere a cardboard box appeared in the middle of the room, with some newspaper in the bottom. "I'm sure you can figure it out. I want wallets, jewelry, all of it. Cooperate, or I'll pry those rings off your cold, dead fingers."

He made eye contact with each and every one of them, pointing to them and then to the box. Ralph and Bob reluctantly threw their wallets into the box, and the ladies worked slowly to take off their least important piece of jewelry. Why bother? They clearly had him outnumbered—unless you count the weapons.

"People?" The Uniform said. "Do you think I'm playing here? I promise you it's much harder to take jewelry off with one of your buddies splattered against the wall. I'm not gonna negotiate every ring and watch with you. I want it all, and I'm gonna get it."

It just wasn't an easy robbery. It was a contrary group. Sarah Joy was flooded with feelings—it was her job to do something. She was afraid, but also outraged that he was doing this. "Please go away," was all she could come up with.

"In a minute, girly," he said. "When I leave is up to you. That's a nice ring you got there. You can make a contribution to my poor box." He flicked his cigarette ashes onto the floor one last time and dropped his smoke into the wine glass that was closest to him.

Sarah Joy's ring—crap. Of course, she had to be wearing the ring her aunt had bought her when they went to Ireland. It was only a silver Celtic knot. It was rich-looking, but not worth much. Still, it was made for her— they had had a silversmith make it in Dunshaughlin and mail it to her.

"This ring isn't worth much, but ..." Sarah Joy began.

"LADY! Focus here. I'm not doing appraisals. You take it off, I take it home, and you become real sad and inconvenienced. I make out like a bandit. See how that works? I don't need a personal story with each item," he growled.

Fine, she said to herself, *but you won't get the hats.*

Bob reached in and took his wallet back. "I don't really use my wallet. I just keep my money in my pocket." He pulled four twenties out of his pocket and threw them in.

"You must think people with guns are fucking stupid," The Uniform yelled. "I'm a professional here. I make observations; it's my job. I knew both you guys had wallets in your back pockets before you knew I was here. You don't take the time to carry an empty wallet! Maybe we should look inside! I'll break one finger for every credit card in there!" Bob knew this was a discussion he was going to lose. "Buy thinner wallets—they don't leave

213

a big old bulge. The cash *and* the wallet, buddy! Now!"
Bob did as he was told.

Bob desperately wanted to make a vacuum pump comment since the topic of big bulges had popped up, but he decided to save it for later.

Sarah Joy looked around the room. Ralph was essentially out on the floor, Millie was against the wall, hurting a bit, and Suzy was in a panic over Ralph's injury. Bob was fine with just giving the guy what he wanted. Sarah Joy and Miss Florrie were not as happy with the situation. Sarah Joy noticed Miss Florrie's cane in the corner farthest from them. She made eye contact with Miss Florrie, then turned her head and looked at the cane again. Too far away; it couldn't work. Miss Florrie noticed a reflection in the mirror—movement. Down the short hallway to the storage room, she saw someone. It was William. (How long had he been there?) Why he never came out when Miss America visited we may never know. He just didn't know what to do. His cell phone was in the pocket of his coat, which hung by the front door, and that was the only option that he could think of through the panic.

When the shotgun had fired in his direction, he wasn't hit, but immediately passed out, and now he was just coming around thanks to the smell of cigarette smoke.

He looked at Miss Florrie. He was embarrassed to imagine that she would have more of a chance than he would to neutralize The Uniform, but he wouldn't know where to begin.

Sweat was dripping off his brow and he had tears in his eyes. He was holding a professional-grade plunger, which is a requirement when William is around. It was the closest thing to a weapon he could find, but he didn't know what to do with it.

Miss Florrie looked at Sarah Joy and nodded her head in the direction of the cane. They looked at each other, and it was clear. Miss Florrie wanted Sarah Joy to get the cane. As The Uniform was pulling a ring off Suzy's finger, Miss Florrie held three fingers up to her chest and counted off—three, two, one.

Sarah Joy stood up and attempted to run across the room, reaching for the cane. Mr. Uniform dropped Suzy's hand and pushed Sarah Joy off her feet and up against the wall. Miss Florrie felt bad about using Sarah Joy as a diversion, but Miss Florrie had gotten up when Sarah Joy had, and moved to the middle of the room, undetected. No one, not even The Uniform, knew what "William, give it to me now!" meant. The industrial-strength plunger flew through the room and into Miss Florrie's open hand. The Uniform tried to move quickly from Sarah Joy to Miss Florrie, taking a swing at the old woman in the process. This time he wasn't so effective. He thought she had ducked down to avoid his swing, but Miss Florrie was squatting down on purpose. She was down like a football player, in a tiny little three-point stance, with the plunger braced between her hands.

"Aaaaahhhhhh!"

A noise came out of Miss Florrie as her body took off. Zero to sixty in five feet! She was a Jaguar. A 'Vette. A Beamer. The Uniform was so surprised to hear her that he didn't even realize what was happening. She was so low that at first he didn't see where she went. This gave her the two hundred milliseconds that she needed. The plunger on the front of this freight-train-in-a-purple-dress came up under the gun barrel, knocked it out of his hand, and sent it flying to the wall. The plunger moved on to his neck and locked under his chin, but it didn't stop.

She was still accelerating! At maximum speed, her feet left the ground.

She T-boned him.

The noise of the crash echoed through The Conscilience as Miss Florrie rode The Uniform through the window behind him and onto the lawn outside. The Uniform weighed about 240 pounds, but he wasn't in great physical shape. When Miss Florrie realized she was going to be in for quite a ride, she changed her grip from the plunger to his two shirt pockets. He slammed down hard, and she landed on top of him, bounced noticeably, and laid there on his chest, but not for long.

When they hit the ground, suddenly a shot rang out.

Miss Florrie got up, like Batman, before anyone could get to her. Blood dripped off the tip of her nose from the six-inch cut down the middle of her smooth, bald head. A piece of her wig hung from a bloody piece of glass in the splintered window four feet above her. Miss Florrie was damn proud of herself.

Time stopped for Sarah Joy. She looked up at the largely smashed window. She smiled, staring at that one piece of glass that remained in the top part of the window frame, sticking down almost like an icicle. It had a red tip covered with blood, and hanging from it was a clump of gray hair. This was important. She'd seen this years before. It *had* meant something!

William passed out for a moment, again, his head eventually sitting on a cardboard box covered in his own sweat. Most of the group never understood that he was actually there.

Sarah Joy jumped up and down and cheered.

Bob was thankful he had worn his brown pants.

Millie looked disgusted with herself for not saving the day. She pulled a knife out of her pocket, and Laurie helped her cut the cords from some blow dryers and used them to tie The Uniform's hands and feet.

William, who finally came to and ventured out of his hiding place, insisted that he accompany Miss Florrie in the ambulance that came for her. He would go so Sarah Joy could stay in the salon, which was now rapidly being taped off as a crime scene. On the drive to the emergency room, William held Miss Florrie's hand. She squeezed his hand tight and talked to him the whole way. She wasn't going to let this night get away from her without understanding what "sucks" means. While William wasn't the best person to ask, he was honest, and she arrived at the emergency room with a smirk on her face.

The doctor told Miss Florrie she needed to keep the wig off for fourteen days to go along with the fourteen stitches she got. It was a good thing, because that wig was history. Sarah Joy worked tirelessly on Monday to order a duplicate for her.

The doctor also suggested that Miss Florrie get weekly massages for a few months because of all the small aches and pains she had following the episode. She became William's first regular client. Helen decided to join her. William's third client was Leonard, a high school teacher.

One of the police officers asked Sarah Joy out.

Sarah Joy said no.

Miss Florrie was asked to speak before the Women's Auxiliary of the American Legion after the story came out in the paper. Thirty-four ladies—Helen was one of them—and sixty-three "mature" men attended. It was a good turnout. Miss Florrie gave a motivational talk: "Take action. If you're sick, attend to it. Find experts. Never stop taking care of yourself. She told them a hair-raising story. She even read to them things like "For hair loss, use cantaloupe." She researched the story of Staciana Stitts, the Olympic swimmer who swam bald—having lost all of her hair to alopecia. Miss Florrie shared with the crowd a quote from Staciana:

> "When I was young, of course not having hair was horrible, but now I can say I'm an Olympian. I feel pretty good about myself. Good enough to be hairless and stand tall and proud. It's a good feeling. When I smile, lots of other people smile!"

At the American Legion Hall, Miss Florrie shared every detail of her emotions on the subject when she spoke, and did it bald. At the end of the meeting, over tea and biscuits, everyone was invited to touch and feel her stitches. She sat quietly, hands folded, in the middle of the room—like a head on a table. All ninety-seven guests touched her. Thirteen asked her out. She wasn't as shy as Sarah Joy in her decisions.

Sarah Joy's carpenter got The Conscilience looking as good as new in a few days. He asked Sarah Joy out.

She said no.

Millie saw Laurie three times, and decided that, while Laurie's body excited her, Laurie's personality was not very attractive. Still, she saw her one last time.

Leonard, the high school teacher and generally nice guy stopped Sarah Joy halfway through his haircut. He reached up and gently grabbed her hand with the scissors in it, and asked if she would go to dinner with him on the weekend.

Sarah Joy said yes.

Sarah Joy cried and cried when Miss Florrie died, but she was not too sad to demand her hat and cane from Miss Florrie's daughter. Sarah Joy slipped a marble into Miss Florrie's casket. Even more upset was Ralph, who went to the funeral but could not approach the casket. He just couldn't do it. He felt totally responsible for her death— and he was!

She had arrived late to a softball game in which that Ralph and Suzy's team was playing. Ralph had hit that ball like he never had before. He watched it sail over the fence—his first home run. He watched people cheering in the crowd. He saw Miss Florrie, both hands in the air, yelling loudly, excited at Ralph's smash hit. While Ralph watched in horror, it appeared that Miss Florrie never knew exactly where the ball was, so she was still cheering when it fell from the sky and slammed into her still-healing scar. At least this time, her wig remained intact. Miss Florrie died happy—out in the fresh air with her new friends, free to cheer at the top of her lungs. It was yet another good day for her, but not so much for her date, who was sitting beside her. For him, it was a very bad first date.

- (15) -

POSTSCRIPT
Later That Night || Flashback

The night of the botched robbery, after Miss Florrie became a superhero; after the EMTs put some temporary bandages on her cuts, and checked bruises on many of the others; after William accompanied Miss Florrie in the ambulance; after everyone who was left hugged everyone else; after Millie (now gunless) drove off; after Bob and wife drove down the road; after Ralph and Suzy left, deciding to follow Miss Florrie's ambulance; and after the police asked a few final questions of Sarah Joy and also asked that she not touch anything until the crime scene investigators could come and decide what they needed, Sarah Joy knew she needed to end this party. There's always an end to her parties, and obviously she's well trained at emptying a room when she wants to!

Sarah Joy ducked under the crime-scene tape that was across her salon doorway and sat down in her barber chair, alone. She slowly spun it around and, for the next few hours, looked at the broken glass with the bloody hair hanging from it. She didn't need to be hit over the head to get it. This was the end of a period in her life—a chapter break. A point where she could relax for a second, contemplate what had happened so far in her life, and start the next chapter, with its own direction.

She felt so fortunate. She thought back to her horrible interview with Diane Grim, and how she had explained that, one way The Conscilience is unique is that all of the clients are nice people. It was a stupid thing to say, but she knew that the ordinary people she took care of every day all did have something in common. She decided that perhaps any good overview of her world would have to include the words "honesty" and "family." She had surrounded herself with people who weren't afraid to speak their minds—not afraid to act, to do what they believed was the right thing, no matter what the consequences. And they did this for two reasons. One was that, of course, they had no choice. It was part of who they were. But the other reason why they did what they did was that they shared a sense of family. After all, if you can't be free to speak your mind, to do what you feel is right, with your family, who can you do it with? They will, after all, always understand. It's what families do. Sarah Joy didn't even consider how she might have contributed to this feeling of family, and love. She just does what she does because she, as well, has no choice. She did feel that she had created something—The Conscilience—and what she had created was good. She was glad she had the moment to think about the big picture, and felt very fortunate.

Her tired eyes, which continued to focus on the broken, bloody glass in her window, watched the wedge of glass occasionally glow for her, then go dark. Twice this happened. The first time was when it was hit by the headlights of a car that had pulled into her parking lot. The second time was when a flashlight approached. Sarah Joy's eyes refocused to see Alicia standing outside, looking in, with a police officer standing behind her.

"Hi," Alicia said.

"Are you OK, ma'am?" the officer asked.

"I'm fine, officer. Thank you. How are you doing, Alicia? Long night?"

Alicia smiled. "The cops hauled me off to the cop shop. I got fingerprinted, and a few detectives got statements from me. It's been a great night!

"My coat, keys, and car are still here," Alicia continued.

"Oh," Sarah Joy said, getting up. "I'm so sorry. I completely forgot. Come on in. Thank you, officer, for bringing her back here. Is there anything else you need?"

"No, just wanted to make sure Crash here is OK. She did call her parents, so they know she'll be late. I talked to them too, so they know what's been happening."

The officer looked at his watch. "It's only 3:30 AM," he said.

"Mom wasn't all that surprised. Dad sounded like he just scored, he's so excited. They're pretty funny … for adults I mean," Alicia explained.

"Well come on in for a minute, 'Crash'," Sarah Joy said, "I've got some cherry coke and a bathroom here you might be interested in."

"Oh, God, am I," Alicia replied.

Much to Sarah Joy's surprise, Alicia hugged the officer, thanked him. He smiled warmly. It was clear she had become the station darling in her short time there.

Sarah Joy sat down on the front room floor, since of course there was no place to sit because no one should ever be waiting. Alicia collapsed to the floor and laid on her back.

Looking up at the ceiling, Alicia said, "I think I like hanging with adults more than kids. I wish I'd understood this earlier! Your friends are all really nice."

"And I hope you understand that you're one of them," Sarah Joy smiled.

"Thanks," Alicia replied, blushing a bit. "You know, I wish I could tell every kid in therapy—if you get one chance to, uh, I don't know, to whack just one person you dislike as hard as you can—all of those complicated feelings that make your life suck just go poof into the air. God, I feel good, and God, that creep Calluna deserved it."

"Well, technically I can't support any kind of violence. We need to learn to be nonviolent. But, Alicia, she might have killed me. And she might not have stopped with me! You saved our lives!" Sarah Joy said.

"I know. What a deal. Two for one. Is life good or what?" Alicia beamed.

"Why don't you go home, baby?" Sarah Joy said. "The sun will be coming up soon."

"Why is everyone all of a sudden calling me 'baby'?" Alicia asked.

"I have absolutely no idea," Sarah Joy replied, "but it just feels right!"

"It does! But I feel older now, not younger!" Alicia agreed.

They both laughed.

They eventually stood up. Sarah Joy got one of those very new Alicia hugs, which felt exceptionally good. Sarah Joy handed her a marble.

"Here. Keep this. I'll explain it to you next time you come in," Sarah Joy said.

Alicia walked to the door slowly, untying a wrist bracelet that she had made, woven out of brown string with a few beads on it. She handed it to Sarah Joy, smiled, and out she went.

Sarah Joy scribbled a note, having just decided that her stationery would now include the new salon philosophy:

THE CONSCILIENCE
Live in the moment
celebrate this day
always look forward to tomorrow
as family

Excerpt from the police report:

Witnesses present reported hearing a gunshot as the woman with the plunger and the perpetrator hit the ground. The perpetrator's gun was knocked out of his hand, and there was no evidence that it accidentally fired when it landed. One witness did have a small handgun, with no license to possess or carry. It had not been fired either. (The decision was made to not pursue this violation at this time.) The ambulance staff treated the perpetrator for a number of bruises and contusions due to the fall, and also for extensive bleeding in a sensitive spot. An investigation of the scene suggests a surprising but simple explanation for these events. When the pair landed, the handle end of the plunger penetrated the soft ground, where there was a small box buried. It contained a single .22 caliber bullet. The impact detonated the bullet. The bullet exited the box on roughly an eighty-two-degree angle, striking the perpetrator's scrotum, which explains the excessive bleeding and complaints of pain. There were also two bullet holes found in the dress of the woman with the plunger. The buried bullet apparently winged said scrotum then passed safely between the woman's legs, entering and exiting her dress without personal injury. The owner of the salon remains to be interrogated to determine if she had any knowledge of ammunition in the lawn.

Alicia left, and Sarah Joy immediately fell asleep on the floor. She didn't have time to realize how exhausted she was. She had no idea how long she'd been asleep, but she was certain that she heard footsteps on the porch and the door open. Sarah Joy rolled over and tried to reach for the cane, two feet away, on the floor. She saw a shadow looming over her. She looked up and was relieved to see it was Alicia.

"I do *not* want this night to end!" Alicia declared. "Come with me. We should go see how Miss Florrie's doing! I'll even drive."

And off they both went, on their adrenalin highs, now knowing that a new adventure can find you at any time, even when the sun is just rising on a new chapter of your life, on a very new day.